WOMEN OUT OF WATER

SHORT STORIES

SALLY CRANSWICK

modjaji books

Published in 2021 by Modjaji Books
Cape Town, South Africa
www.modjajibooks.co.za

Edited by Karen Jennings
Cover artwork by Jesse Breytenbach
Text design and typesetting by User Friendly
Set in Bembo Std 11 on 14 pt

ISBN print 978-1-928433-25-5
ISBN ebook 978-1-928433-26-2

CONTENTS

HORSE

Let us start, for both our wills, joined now, are one.
You are my guide, you are my lord and teacher.
These were my words to him and, when he moved,
I entered on that deep and rugged road.

Dante, *The Divine Comedy, Vol. I: Inferno*;
Canto II; 141

Solitude is the profoundest fact of the human condition.
Man is the only being who knows he is alone.

Octavio Paz, *The Labyrinth of Solitude*

The man put the rug on its back. The young horse's flesh twitched, turning teeth to flanks, sweat forming on his shoulders. And from the veranda, shaded by the jacaranda tree that flourished there in the summer months, Alma could see the fear in her son's eyes.

This was the moment when he would realise if he had wasted their money or spent it wisely on a good bloodline. Two years of waiting had come to this and he was aware; aware of the physical danger from the stallion and the emotional danger of losing any reputation he had gained through late-night whisky talk.

Alma watched the horse. The legs of a thoroughbred, narrow enough to snap at the fetlock, tapering to elegant knees, his coat blacker than the sun-worn backs of the farm workers. As he sidestepped and pranced on light, unshod hooves through the sand, she let her eyes run over the lines of muscle and realised at three years old he was easily the biggest horse they'd had on the farm and when he filled there would be more to come. Watching that balled-up power was a potent reminder of what she had lost.

She knew the fight both man and horse were about to enter and, unable to watch, she turned her head to the west. The air was dry. It carried cool winds from central Africa and with them the dust that invaded her home. Coarse brown dust lay on her kitchen table so that when she polished she sanded, year after year, renewing the oak grain. She put her hand to her face and drew her finger through the deep lines that ran along the sides of her mouth, let her fingertips glide over the wrinkles etched at the corner of her eyes and ran the fleshy part of her forefinger in a straight line down the middle of her brow, feeling the furrow that had become her dominating feature.

She called Nsousa. Tea would come presently. Sometimes they shared a cup, but they had nothing much left to say to each other after all these years. They were just two old ladies with dwindling families.

There was a sharp cry which returned her gaze to the paddock. Her son was in the sand, rubbing his thigh. Patches of crimson rising into angry circles on his cheeks as he stood. He gripped both sides of the head-collar, using his bodyweight against the animal. The stallion shook his head and moved backwards on low hindquarters, dragging Callum as he edged closer to the fence. It had become a game of brute strength – something Alma had taught him never to enter into with a horse.

There was a high-pitched whinny before the animal lowered his head to his knees and sprang up, crashing his bony poll into

Callum's jaw. Her son, once again, lay struggling in the sand. As he paused to catch his breath, the horse settled. If Callum knew it, this was the moment he could regain control; the horse was still prepared to give him another chance. The great animal exhaled soft grunts as his ribs rose and fell with his breath. He took several small steps back through the sand, watching and waiting. Callum only saw the challenge of the unbroken animal and swore as he reached behind him to grab the long training whip.

Using his flight or fright instinct, the horse, with flared nostrils and eyes rolling, jack-knifed into the air and bucked all the way to the edge of the paddock. As he leapt, the backing-rug flew off him, and before it had even landed in the red dirt, the horse had galloped, churning dust clouds behind him, to the boundary of the ménage and Alma saw what he was capable of as the animal powered down into his haunches, lifted his front legs high into the air, stretched his neck out into a perfect arc and cleared the barbed-wire fence with inches to spare. In one leap, the horse had become free-range.

With two-thousand hectares for him to roam in, it could take days to track him. He could join the small zebra herd or run with the buck for a while. It was clear he would not be running back to her son's hands.

Callum was looking at her now and she averted her eyes. No point in denting his male ego further. Nsousa silently manoeuvred the tea things into place and shuffled into the kitchen.

He was a weak boy. He looked strong enough, but the person he wanted to be shadowed everything he did. Unsure of his place in society, feeling the need to be accepted and yet, feeling too different to fit in. Alma always thought if he had been brought up somewhere else, where the need to be a man was less prevalent, he might have made a success of himself. But the refusal to leave was ruining him. And that was not something you could tell a son. Ironically, he blamed her, as children who do not want to recognise their own failings are apt to do with their mothers.

She watched her son abandoning the paddock and heading for the stables. No doubt concocting a story for his father in which others were to blame for this latest misfortune.

The heat had a sound of its own, a hazy, static crackle accompanied by noon noises: cicadas, the swish of the dairy cattle's tails, the drone from the ever-present flies, Nsousa clattering her way slowly around the kitchen.

She collected her cane from the side of her chair and stood up. Bones and wasted muscles protested. She took her time, waiting for her body to become fully erect, and thought of the stallion and the leap he had taken. She had tamed many wild horses, but this one was different. He was neither vicious nor lazy, as stallions can be. She had watched him roaming the enclosures, making contact with the mares, the workers. A horse like that would do well in the right hands and if he made stud grade they might be able to pay back what they owed on the farm. Then there would be something to sell, she could move to a flat in town and she would not have to die in this hot place.

But a good stud horse needed to have education as well as bloodline. No one would pay for a rogue stallion to cover valuable mares. No one would risk a brood mare breaking its back against the best stud stallion in the world.

She stepped off the veranda and began her slow walk over the lawn towards the stables. Using her cane for support, she took care over the patchy buffalo grass. Once manicured to perfection, it now straggled menacingly around the perimeter of the garden, host to alien grasses and grainy ant-heaps. The sharp grasses caught hold of bare flesh and dug in, to remind that a real African grass, even a domesticated one, was an element that one should be wary of.

She no longer took painkillers for her knee. She embraced the pain – more of a discomfort these days now that she was used to it. It meant that on the better days she could imagine the injury was healing and her body was finally renewing itself. Physical pain was far easier to endure than psychological pain. Thoughts could drive a person to madness. And she had fought against that slow demise since that morning, when her men had set out against her wishes, without her.

She entered the stable block. The smell of horses always comforting: the sweet glycerine of saddle soap, aromatic bridle leather – smells that reminded her of her younger self. The show bell ringing, the push of heels into the double, legs quickening under her. She had always pushed to the limit and took the risks needed. Everyone questioned how the tiny woman from the southern province found winning horse after winning horse, but she knew that winning horses were not found, they were made.

'What're you doing over here?' Callum asked, the smell of Rothmans still on him.

She felt pity. A man of forty shouldn't be stuck with two old parents and a few members of staff that remembered him in nappies. He stayed on to make things better, but with each failed attempt he became increasingly bitter. 'Just go!' she wanted to scream at him. 'Find happiness.' But the words would sound accusing.

'Wondered if you need any help?'

'Don't think so.' He glanced at her leg. 'Thanks all the same, Ma.'

'And the horse?' she couldn't help asking.

'Bloody animal.' He lit a cigarette, drew deeply on it. 'He'll get hungry. Then I'll get him right. He'll pay me what he owes me. Plus some.'

Where had he learnt such ignorance towards a green beast? Alma had taught him to ride – he had watched her training horses from his pram, and yet no imprint had been left on him.

'Well, if you do need me…' but she trailed off, seeing his

undisguised expression. The look of youth that tries to mask its revolt from frailty, as though age were a disease one could catch.

That evening, she lay in bed alone, her husband on another trip. Where he went to at his age, she had no idea, but he had come and gone throughout their marriage and she enjoyed the peace of his absence in such a way that she never thought to question or detain him.

She always liked to sleep with the windows wide open so the air could reach into the room. The night sounds made up a part of her dreams: deep owl hoots, restless baboons, scratching porcupines, the frogs calling out to defend territory. There was nothing that held fear for her in this lonely bush. And as the scent of night jasmine crept into her half-sleep, she knew what dawn would bring for her.

She put the essentials into a green canvas bag, which she hung diagonally over her shoulder. There was a fresh chill in the morning air which would offer relief until the hot day settled in. It was still dark, but she did not mind, she had navigated the farm many times without light.

With her cane, she set out to the perimeter fence, to where the horse had made its exit. His tracks were easy to find; strong, angry marks in the ground which headed straight into the bush. His direction was north and the thought made her shiver. If he kept on this route, he would come to the koppies. Like an unwelcome love note, she folded the thought away. She needed to reach the horse before anyone else did.

The house was on a higher point than the surrounding bush and, from where she stood, she could see trees silhouetted black against the ochre haze of the horizon. The low-lying bush sprawled in front of her, merging with the higher, more thinly-spread acacia in the distance. It was a long time since she had set out alone in the bush.

She had no way of knowing how far he had gone or how long her journey would take, but the horse had been out to grass until recently and he would tire quickly in this terrain and heat. A horse will stay close to home, even when on the loose. They are not solitary creatures by habit and when he finally settled and forgot what he was running from, he would stay where he was until he found a herd to join or a mare to dominate.

She looked up into the early-morning sky and rested her eye on the North Star, milky and opaque in its dying hour. But checking her direction was not necessary. She knew which way was north.

Her body was no longer a thing she could trust and she knew her knee would not hold out through the twisted acacia scrub. If she took the old truck track which ran through the middle of the farm to the cattle station, she could keep the stallion's spoor to her left and turn off only when she had to.

'I hope you haven't gone too far into that thicket, boy,' she thought to herself. 'It's been a long time since I've tracked a beast and the way you jumped that fence…' Her thought trailed as she remembered the animal stretched in the perfect equine arc.

She looked down at her legs, thin through the corduroy of her trousers, her knee turned slightly outwards as usual, but this morning, for the first time, it occurred to her that it made her look comical.

'Sorry, horse,' she said softly, the sibilance of her voice coming back to her in the dense morning air. 'It's not a very grand party setting out to fetch you.' She poked her stick into the ground in front of her. 'But you might be pleased of that in any case.'

She leant heavily into her stick. She moved first her right leg then her left, slowly finding the rhythm she had developed over time. Cane down, hip up, swing knee out, foot down.

Cane, hip, knee, foot.

Cane, hip, knee, foot.

The farmhouse behind her was silent and she did not turn to look at it as she made her way forward. Nsousa would be there presently and she had a feeling the old maid would leave her be.

The ground was dry and hard. Red, crumbling soil dusted the surface. The trucks had left deep grooves over the years and she had to be careful not to lose her footing, but she wanted to travel as far as possible in this half-light. She used to love riding and walking at dawn; the light gave her a feeling that she was floating over the ground, ephemeral, ghostly, and she was surprised at how immediate the memory was to her.

When she first came from the city, she had found the bush to be a silent place, punctuated by a rumbling truck or a cattle bell. That was until she heard her first dawn chorus. She used to get up in the shift between night and day – even when she did not have to – just to revel in the noise that shut out all other sounds and, for some time in her life, it had been enough to shut away her thoughts too.

As Alma made her way through the farm, she listened for the calls she knew, as if listening to an orchestra. Down at the bottom with the bass notes was the bush shrike's whistle, low and mournful, the waxbill's tune cut through the middle notes, harsh and nasal, and then there was the solo appearance of the cuckoo finch, high and rasping. She saw it flit through her eyeline and land on a thorn bush to her right. It watched her through a dark liquid eye. With its shocking yellow markings against the faun of the bush, it had been one of the first birds Alma noticed on the farm. But she had read it was a parasitic bird that laid eggs in other birds' nests and its hatchlings trampled the host chicks to death in their quest for life.

'You can look at me,' she said aloud, 'but that doesn't make us friends.' The bird hopped into the air and disappeared behind the branches.

A go-away bird called out like a part of the violin chorus and she knew it was a warning: beware, old woman approaching.

Alma rarely walked far these days and the burden of carrying her stick began to weigh on the muscles of her shoulders and back. It was a part of her now and she couldn't remember the last time she had tried to walk without it. The handle, smooth in her hands, moulded to her shape, both friend and foe.

Not thirty minutes had passed and she had to stop. Leaning against a boulder, she bent over to rub her knee. The joint was cold and numb and she tried to massage it with her old fingers. If she allowed the blood to stop flowing, she knew the swelling would come, making progress impossible.

'Come on, body, this is no time to let me down,' she said aloud, surprised at the sound of her own voice. It had a throaty crackle to it and it was louder than she had intended. It was the unmistakable sound of an old woman.

'I must stay positive,' she thought. 'If I ignore the knee, there is a good chance the pain will go away.' But whichever way she tried to walk, the rutted track drew her feet into it, turning her ankles, putting pressure on her knee and hips. There was no flat ground.

Except for the bush.

Under the cover of the shoulder-high bush, the soil was softer and damper. It would be easier underfoot, but trekking through the trees would mean bending and stretching, things she had avoided for too many years. She also knew that spiders liked to spin invisible webs between the branches and wait for their prey to cross before injecting them with venom. Cobras slept in the low branches and puffadders liked the cool shade of the tree roots to await mealtimes. Scorpions could be anywhere – wooden hollows, decaying scrub, their sting poisonous enough to finish an old woman within an hour.

There had been a black mamba in Nsousa's hut when her little boy was the same age as Matthew. They didn't know how many nights the snake had been coiled in the rafters above Dembe's bed whilst he slept. When Nsousa discovered it, they had all abandoned the home and none of the farm workers were willing to enter the hut to remove one of the world's most venomous snakes.

Alma had poked a rifle through the grass thatch, but the snake had taken to the warmth of the loft as a result of all the commotion. With Nsousa adamant that she would never return with the risk of a snake in her home, there was nothing left to do. Alma hauled out all Nsousa's possessions herself before dousing the rondavel in petrol and throwing a flaming torch through the doorway. She held Nsousa's child tight as he wept for his home, kissing his soft hair, wiping his eyes.

The witch doctor came to bless the ground before they built Nsousa another hut. Dembe had grown into a tall, strong man and, as soon as he turned seventeen, he left them to find work in Johannesburg. The day he left was the only time Alma ever held Nsousa. She held her so that she could feel her bosoms press against her and she kissed the top of her head, the hair soft and coiled, the gentle aroma of coconut strange in her nostrils.

She bent to pull her socks over the bottom of her trousers. The bush had grown over since she had last been here. The route would be less clear. At least she would be closer to the horse's tracks. Soon enough, others would start looking for the horse in their trucks, carrying ropes and darts. Her options were limited; there were only two routes to choose from.

The relief of softer ground almost made her knee feel youthful. She kept her bearing northwards, towards the koppies and the horse. The morning chill was wearing off and her activity warming her up. She unzipped her oilskin jacket.

Her progress with the cane was slow. She concentrated on the rhythm.

Cane, hip, knee, foot.

Cane, hip, knee, foot.

The tailing off of birdsong. The quietness of early morning.

Cane, hip, knee, foot.

'I must look ridiculous,' she thought. 'Like a stuffed doll in the hands of a toddling child.' And then she wondered, 'If I was a doll, would they throw me away or try to mend me?'

As a young woman she had walked out to the koppies many times, collecting stray calves, rounding up her free horses, and she had never taken longer than four hours to get there on foot, but when she took the children, she had driven. Children, even boys, she discovered, do not like to walk for hours.

During the spring months they had insisted she take them to the koppies to search for treasures, always hoping the rain had washed enough soil away to unearth the trinkets they hunted every year.

She gave them each an old bully beef can – even Matthew, although she always knew she would end up carrying it for him – and she took them to the base of the koppies in the truck. There was a song they used to sing on the way, the older boys in the open truck, her baby next to her in the cab, but she could not remember what it was now.

Hundreds of years ago, traders from North Africa passed through the farm on their way to Southern Africa. They camped on the high ground of the koppies, taking advantage of the water and game, perhaps stopping for a few days at a time to stock up before moving on to sell their goods to the colonisers who craved the exotic spices, fabrics, jewels and earthenware that could be theirs so easily in this plentiful continent. Whenever they moved off, they dropped little pieces of their livelihood in the soil which, over the years, had been covered with the shifting landscape. It was these things the boys sought – a brightly-coloured bead, a spice bag, a piece of cut glass, a tool.

They never found treasure of any kind, but the boys never gave up their search and their hope was a quality she admired. They scratched with fingers, hand forks and trowels, turned over rocks they must have moved hundreds of times, and at each turn she could see the anticipation on their faces. Perhaps this stone, perhaps this tree root, perhaps this ant heap.

She used to imagine the joy it would bring them to find something after all their searching. There would have been such a celebration in the truck on the way home.

At the pace she was going now, it would be evening before she arrived at the koppies.

Cane, hip, knee, foot.

Cane, hip, knee, foot.

She thought of the horse and how he would be coping in this terrain. His fine body was not used to the rough bush or the harsh sun on his back. Her own horses always had a free run before she brought them in for training; it toughened them and gave them common sense, but this horse had been stabled, hand fed and his good sense taken away from him at an early age. She had to get to him before the bush did. An unmoulded beast, fresh and green, would meld with this environment quickly and in a short time it would be too difficult for her to work him.

The heat was coming now and she tied her jacket around her waist. She hardly felt the thorns ripping at her flesh. Like parchment paper, soft and old, the skin drew away from her body, drawing red-ink lines on her forearms.

Perhaps it was the warmth of the sun on old joints, perhaps it was her blood flowing more freely, but as she moved through the bush, concentrating on the horse, her body began to loosen. She didn't even notice that she was using her stick to swipe away tendrils of vine, to poke old man's beard from her path and to move aside loose stones.

She stopped for a moment, leaning on a stump of fallen tree, her breath hard, her heart beating. As soon as the beating levelled out, she moved off again and it was a few moments until she realised she was moving with a new rhythm.

'Ha!' she laughed out loud, stopping and holding the stick in front of her. 'I'm not even using you anymore, old friend. In fact,' she said, shaking the stick, 'are you supporting me, or am I supporting you?'

She bent to pick up a sandstone rock with one hand. When she was erect, she poked the ground with her stick, searching for a softer piece of turf. When she found the right spot, she placed the cane firmly on the soil and hammered it into the ground with the rock, smooth and hard in her hand. She stood back from her work, sweat on her forehead and under her arms. The stick, upright in the soil, its dark-wood handle curved at the top, looked like a simple bush grave.

'Here rests Alma's stick,' she said. 'Back to the land it came from.' She stood upright and crossed herself, feeling light-headed and with energy she hadn't known for years. It was as if her body had followed her mind into another place where they connected to make up a younger person, free of disability and age.

'I'm coming for you, horse,' she said as she tightened her hat strap under her chin and she began the second part of her journey through the higher, more thinly-spaced acacia trees.

It didn't occur to her that she might need the stick later. The freedom that came with the rejection of it overtook her.

She continued her journey northwards, no quicker than before, but without the cane-hip-knee-foot action her movement felt smoother and less intrusive in the bush. After all this time of resenting her body and allowing it to hinder her, she felt they were finally working towards a common goal.

To find the horse.

To bring him home.

To put ghosts to rest.

The sun was burning through the trees onto her hat and through to her scalp. Her body was damp with the heat and the bag was making a dent in her shoulder. Her feet, unused to such movement, were beginning to blister at the heels. She knew from the high sun that it was midday and that reminded her she had not eaten since before first light.

'If I don't eat then I'll be good for nothing,' she thought, as she found a flat rock and sat on it. She stretched out her legs and rubbed them from the thighs down to the ankles before unbuckling her bag. She unwrapped a plain bread roll from a piece of sandwich paper and, tearing a piece off, she began to chew carefully. Old teeth need time to work and caution came as second nature to her.

The birds were completely still now. Nothing much moved at this time of day. Cicadas, lizards, a short burst through dry undergrowth. Perhaps it was the silence, but she was not unused to that. Perhaps it was the walk, but she'd walked the farm many times over and had always managed to cut off thoughts before they fully surfaced. Perhaps it was her age. Yes, that was probably it. An old woman alone in the bush was bound to start thinking to herself. About mistakes she had made. About decisions she had never made. And about how some things happen in life and there is just no controlling them.

When she'd arrived it had been the dry season. That whole week she had slept badly, not sure if it was down to the extreme heat or the extreme isolation. When she had discussed the move with Kent, she'd had a romantic notion of what life in Africa would be like. And then, as her life started to slide out of control – the issues she was facing with her job, the sudden death of her brother, her parents' grief, her own grief – moving away seemed like a temporary solution. She hadn't considered that she might never see England again.

She had waited five days to unpack. The red case, newly bought from Peter Jones on the King's Road, rested at the foot of her bed, giving her an uneasy feeling when it caught her eye. Its very newness indicating everything that was naive about her expectations of a remote farm in the middle of Africa.

She'd had one of those nights where dreams weave in and out of consciousness, so that she wasn't sure if she had slept or if the dreams had been real, and as she stood in the kitchen, pouring hot water over tea leaves, she had realised her mistake.

When Kent walked in, she saw him look at her T-shirt and naked legs.

'Perhaps Valerie can tell you where you can get some clothes,' he said, pouring tea.

'I thought money was tight.'

'It is, but I think you might be more comfortable in something less…' a hesitation, 'colourful?'

'I don't think Valerie and I have much in common.'

'I'm making suggestions to help you fit in more.'

'I don't know if I want to fit in more.' The sentence hung between them, like the dog smell, thick in the air.

She saw him glance towards the truck. He was leaving for a cattle sale and she was not sure how long he would be away for.

'I've been wondering. Perhaps I should go back to London – we could both go. I think I made some hasty decisions.'

'Alma,' he almost whispered. The way he said it made her throat ache. 'There isn't the money to go back. I meant it when I said I'd spent everything on this place. Even if I wanted to go back, we can't.'

She let the tears come and even though she didn't want to say it, she did whisper, 'I think I'm lonely here.'

He stroked her hair. 'Give things a chance. It's strange because it's new. You'll get used to it.'

He picked up his shirt. 'Do you want me to stay?'

'No. Your trip has been planned for ages. I'll be okay. Really. There's plenty to do. I'll get stuck in.'

'That's my girl!'

She was surprised that he accepted her answer so readily and she watched him march across the front lawn to the truck, saw two black men get into the back of the cab, and kept watching until long after the dust had settled on the track and the engine noise had faded.

The smell of wet dogs followed her to the bedroom and she opened the red case, threw its contents on the bed and put it on top of the wardrobe, covering it in a thick blanket.

Feeling the wheat bloat her stomach, she rested on the rock and, fanning herself with her hat, she turned her thoughts to the horse.

There is nothing like tracking an animal for building up a picture of it. And from the tracks she had been following she could sense this horse was fleeing. He hadn't slowed up yet; the prints were still strong in the ground and the hoof marks were forward facing, occasionally darting to the side before continuing ahead. He was running fast; he was jumpy from the bush noises. The memories of the farm were still propelling him forwards and she wondered how many times her son had tried to train the horse before she had watched him yesterday.

She finished chewing, took some water and buckled her bag.

In the thinner acacia wood she could move more easily. Without the bending and twisting she was free to enjoy the sensation of walking and using her body for a purpose.

The stallion guided her through the bush and she was grateful for the signposts he left for her. His first dung had been of a dark green liquid and had trailed for several metres before ending, but as he moved on the dung became firmer, and here she could see he had stopped. His dung was a lighter brown and was in a pile. She did not need to touch it to see that it still held warmth. She was closer to him than she dared to hope.

He led her through the bush. When his tracks veered into easier terrain, she followed and so found herself on the smoothest path. If she lost his tracks, she would wait, listen, put her nose to the air and sense him. His pull was visceral; he left a streak of power behind him like a jet's vortex and she picked it up and used it. To track successfully means relying on the senses and she was surprised to find that she, an old woman, was still able to use her senses in such a way.

The sun's intensity was not breaking. She imagined the horse in a shady spot, tail flicking at flies. If she was right, he would be waiting at the entrance to the koppie caves where there was shelter and he felt far enough from the farm for safety. There used to be a water-hole behind the caves and she hoped he would have the sense to find it.

As the trees became more widely spaced and the ground clearer, she was able to look to the horizon for the first time. She could see the koppies at last, hazy in the distance, but she did not stop to look at them. She kept walking. It was only the horse she thought of until she reached the edge of the acacia and looked out to her new path.

From here onwards the ground was rocky. Over the years sandstone chips had drifted from the koppies and scattered out, giving the impression of an alien landscape – moonlike and uncertain. The low-lying shrubs gripped onto life between the rubble, and behind the koppies, way in the distance, the mountain range spread as wide as the horizon. It had no beginning and no end. It loomed into forever, locking life in on both sides. If the horse kept running, Alma supposed he would come to the mountains in time.

'You'll have to stop when you get there though, boy,' she said. 'Even with these new legs, I don't think I will be able to follow you that far.'

The light began to move. No longer on top of her, the sun was dropping from the sky. The stallion's tracks became harder to follow as shadows fell from the rocks. She could see the stony terrain had caused him new panic. His fleshy soles no doubt sore over the unfamiliar rocks. He would feel exposed after the safety of the trees. Alma imagined she was the beast and she imagined she could see the world through his eyes and she saw the only thing that he would see. The cover of the koppies.

She had thought it would be easier going when she reached the open area, but she was slowing down. 'I'll have to take my time over these rocks,' she thought. 'These old legs must be as brittle as kindling wood. If I fall then God knows what fate will await us. An animal could easily break a leg in this territory.' But she calmed her thoughts.

'He will be in the cave; I can feel it strongly.'

'I will find him and I will bring him home.'

She never did manage to bring Mala home. Someone else had done that for her and she could never bring herself to ask who. But this stallion, she would bring home. Even if it killed her.

The land had changed so much; the bush had shifted. It was like new people had moved into her house and changed the furniture and the pictures and it was a home she no longer recognised. There was only a small family of giraffe on the farm, but they could mould the landscape so quickly, pruning the thorn trees, making new tracks to fresher trees and water.

It was Valerie who had first shown her the giraffe. She had arrived in a shiny blue Land Rover and insisted they go for a game drive. On the back seat was a basket with muffins, bread, home-made chutney and a cloth with a blue paisley-pattern on it. As they left, Valerie passed a bag to Alma.

'Just some needles and leftover wool – thought it was time you put yourself to good use, young lady. I knitted our house-boy a vest last month and you should have seen his face when I gave it to him. It was like all his birthdays come at once. Of course, it's not in their culture to say thank you, but I know how grateful he was.'

The morning after, Alma walked to the compound, dragging a bright red object behind her. As she arrived, she saw the central fire burning in a pile. A woman stirred a large pot over it, another was sweeping the dirt between the rondavels with a switch and another, older woman, sat with her back against the perimeter wall, smoking a long pipe.

She reached the middle of the clearing and, seeing nowhere else appropriate, lay the case down and opened it. She pulled out rich colours: silk blouses, dresses, tight-knit jerseys with matching cardigans and costume jewellery.

All movements were stilled and all eyes were on her.

She held up a patent burgundy boot and pointed to a group of dusty, black children crouching over a lizard. 'For them,' she paused in the silence. 'And you too. If you like.'

They looked at her, the women and the children, but no one moved towards her or the case. It lay open on the ground like a body on an operating table, its entrails hanging out.

As she walked back along the path to the house, she could hear movement amongst the group, but she did not turn around. She walked to the homestead with her head up and her back straight.

She was taking her time now and picked her way over the stones, careful to keep her ankles strong and her weight centred. She wanted to make sure she took exactly the same route as the horse. When she found him, she wanted to know the journey he had been on. To have walked in his footsteps would help her understand his behaviour.

Even as the sun dulled, the heat remained. The dry wind moved the air and flicked up dust so Alma had to squint and dip her hat over her brow. She drank from her bottle as she walked in concentration on the path. It was the sound of a vulture that made her look up suddenly.

Then she saw it right there in front of her.

The lightning tree, smooth and silver. At the edge of the old farm track.

A shiver ran over her, but she did not stop in that place, she kept moving although the emotion was coming to her in a way she had never allowed it to before. Her knee ached again, sharp stabs of pain echoing in her leg, moving into her ankles and feet. She took her hat off and ran her fingers through her thick, white hair and wiped her eyes so that she could see the way ahead clearly.

The ragged shadow of the vulture circled her and she looked into the open sky.

'I'm not done yet, so you can go back home!' she shouted into the dense heat. A lonely voice which reached beyond the caves.

A disturbance came back. Loose rocks falling.

So, she had been right.

He was there.

And he had heard her.

The tracks were now too difficult to follow. The horse had run circles, jumped over rocks and boulders and scattered soil and debris behind him. Alma let them go. 'I know where you are, boy,' she thought. 'I'll give myself a break and head straight towards you now. I'll be with you soon and then I might need some strength in these old legs.'

As the heat began to fade at last, the sun settled along the ridge of the distant mountains. She coughed as the dust caught in her throat and she stopped to put on her oilskin. Cracks formed lightning lines along the soil underfoot. The boys had not believed her when she told them of the life waiting underground for the rains to come. Frogs, she had told them, fish, tadpoles, all waiting like Egyptian mummies for the water to quench them into life. The children had wanted to see for themselves so she brought them here. This lower ground was where the pans settled when the rains came and they had all waded barefoot into the ponds, Matthew on her shoulders, looking for life after five days of rain. But all they could find were terrapins, large and moist. Pointed snouts and black eyes floating like crocodiles, sated. Matthew had cried. 'Show me the frogs, Mummy, Matty wants a frog.' The older two had tried to catch a terrapin, but the reptiles snapped into the muddy depths, burying themselves, prepared to wait in dry graves if they had to, until the next feast arrived.

Without the stallion's tracks, she now had to find her own way over the final stretch of scrubland. She tried to place her feet in between the stones but it was difficult for her to keep steady. Some of the fluidity she had discovered through the bush was leaving her as she had to navigate over this strange and rocky territory. As she neared the koppies, the stones were closer together and her feet slipped over them, turning her ankle, jarring her knee, straining her hip.

'Silly old fool thinking you wouldn't need that stick,' she said. Her calf muscles pulled tightly as she took hold of her thigh and lifted her leg over another rock.

The cool wind cut through the end-of-day warmth and she took her hat off whilst she tied her headscarf in place. There was less than a kilometre left to go. 'If I can keep these old legs moving forwards,' she thought, 'then I'll reach the horse before darkness.'

Echoes of her own footsteps called back to her from the caves. The horse would hear her approach. 'That's okay,' she thought. 'The noise will keep him alert, interested in my arrival. He'll be ready for some company now.'

She looked to see if she could trace his outline in the distance, but as she looked up, her foot caught between two rocks and her knee gave way under her.

It happened suddenly and pain shot through her whole leg as she fell to the stony ground. Rock chips knifed their way into the soft skin of her ribs.

'Dammit, you stupid old woman! Pay attention.' Pain ran the length of her body as she lay on her side, breathing in and out, trying to exhale the physical pain from her body.

She let her head rest back, face up to the sky, resigning herself, momentarily, to her predicament.

After a while, the late sun felt good on her face.

'I'm so close to you, horse,' she said. 'Forgive me, because I'm not the woman I used to be. But,' she thought, 'I am a woman, and if there's one thing I know, I have the strength that comes to all of us in our darkest hour. When we most need it.'

Her body had carried life and given birth three times and although she was unable to recall the physical pain of childbirth, she remembered watching each infant take its first breath in the world and how she had searched them with her eyes, taking snapshots in her mind.

Both Peter and Matthew had been early, it was only Callum whom she had carried for two weeks past her due date. It had been high summer and the daytime temperatures were in the forties. The tin roof on the garage crackled and waves shimmered across the lawn. Every day dragged past with the swelling and the nausea which had been with her throughout. There was a point when she thought the child would have to be ripped from her body, until late one night, when Kent had been called out to the cattle station, she started.

There was a storm coming. The closeness was unbearable and Alma lay in her bed pinned down by invisible hands. The child had taken so long to come, it was as if his arrival had been forgotten and so she found herself labouring alone, a sleeping toddler in the next room for company.

The contractions came quickly. Before, she had been eased into them, but now within thirty minutes she was on all fours, panting, feeling the waves spasm through her belly and shoot through her spine. So intense that she had not been able to crawl to the bathroom. She had tried gripping the bed for support, but the sheets slipped through her hands and fell around her. The wooden floor splintered into her knees as she bore down with each new contraction and, even then, she clamped her mouth shut, needing Peter to stay asleep in the next room. She pushed the air so heavily out of her nose that it stung the back of her throat. Warm sticky fluids escaped from her and oozed on the floor, into the sheets. She struggled to escape from them, but each time the contractions arrested her body until her nightie was caked, bloodied and wet, the cold cotton clinging to her thighs. It did not occur to her to try and remove it; all her concentration was centred on the baby, which would surely arrive at any moment.

Were it not for the physical pain, which was so overwhelming that it blotted out reality, she would have cried. Tears of self-pity for a girl who would have chosen to be in a hospital with starched nurses, a concerned husband waiting outside the room and loving parents at the end of a phone.

She banged her forehead against the floor. If she could make it hurt enough it might take away the other pain. But every few minutes the brutality of childbirth rent her body into stiff spasms until she lay exhausted on her side, waiting for the next contraction, gulping, sobbing dry tears, until finally the child was forcing its way out of her, ripping at her, burning a path through her and into the world. It was then that she woke Peter up.

When Kent finally walked into their bedroom all she saw were his boots, thick with mud.

The child was in her arms, still attached to its cord, silent, as he lay for the first time at his mother's breast. The two of them on the floor. Both waiting.

The white egrets gathered overhead, moving from the cattle station to the protection of the trees for the evening. A couple of stray ibis joined them on their short trip, long beaks held regally in front of them. The sun went down quickly in the bush. She had to reach cover before darkness. An old woman lying wasted on the ground would attract unwelcome attention from wild dogs, rogue baboons, mountain lions. She put her hand instinctively to her bag and felt the soft coiled rope inside.

'I'm coming, horse,' she said. 'I'm sorry that I'm only an old woman; perhaps you deserve better.'

And then she thought, 'If I was twenty I would certainly reach the horse quicker, but without my years of learning the journey would be futile. It's not my strength that will bring this horse home. It is my mind. Perhaps the horse will not be sorry after all.'

She tried to roll onto her front, but the rocks sunk in to her flesh.

The only way she could get up was to turn on all fours, wait, then push up onto her knees. Shooting pains. Pause. Lift into a squat. Wait. Push up again from the ground and straighten up her back.

Her head rushed with heat and she fought back silver dots from her vision.

'Be strong, old girl. Not far to go now,' she said as she shuffled towards the koppies.

She could see him standing in the cave entrance, his head outside, his body inside. He looked irritable, jerking his head, moving his hooves. He had traces of foam still on him and, although mostly dry now, she would have liked to rub him over with twined grasses, strap his coat to invigorate circulation and remove the moisture to keep the chill night from him. She wanted to make him comfortable, but to try to get close now would have the opposite effect. He was young, strong; he would cope.

She approached him in the dusk, eyes down, pretending not to see him there. She could feel his stare on her, she could feel his ears twitching at the sound of her steps approaching, now dulled, under the canopy of night.

Nearly there now, she took her time and approached slowly, singing to herself so that he would hear her coming, gradually. A lullaby. One she had sung to her boys before sleep:

Thula, thula, thula, Mtwana
Thula, thula, thula, Mtwana
Ungakhali
Umama akekho
Umama uzobuya.

She heard a deep whinny. He was listening.

The rocks were tangled with gorse and she walked carefully as the night fell heavily around her.

She could no longer see where her feet fell so relied on instinct, the pull of the horse whose musky scent was strong in her nostrils. And softly:

Be still, be still, be still, my child.
Be still, be still, be still, my child.

The animal saw her and leapt back into the cave and she waited, anticipating his next move. Realising he would be trapped there, he panicked, sprang out on all four legs, stones crumbling away beneath uncoordinated limbs as he landed heavily. Eyes wide, nostrils flared, senses alert. And still softly:

Do not cry
Mother is absent
Mother shall come back
Thula, thula, thula, Mtwana
Thula, thula, thula, Mtwana.

Her body became taller. As she moved closer, the horse whinnied. The whinny was long. It began with a high-pitched whine then moved into a deep grumble towards the end.

All the time, his body was bouncing up and down on legs that were working like springs, ready to propel him if he took fright. She could not help thinking that in the right hands and in a controlled environment, he would be performing a perfect dressage movement. He was a horse built for many things.

'It's okay, boy,' she whispered. 'I won't come too close. I'll be here.' And she sat, at the mound of rocks that formed the wider opening of the cave, and looked to the dark horizon, feigning disinterest in the horse. He would feel more at ease with the attention off him for now. They both stayed in position, silently, neither demanding anything from the other.

She looked at him from the corner of her eye. His forelegs were scratched and droplets of congealed blood had collected around his pasterns. The perfect line of his coat was nicked on the shoulders from thorn scratches, some thorns were still sticking out of him, like tiny swords in a matador's bull. But it was all superficial. Nothing broken, no bites, no fever. He was jumpy though. Gaining his trust would not be easy. And she hadn't seen him walk yet. There could be a stone bruise on his sole, lameness she hadn't been able to spot, which would make the walk home a difficult one.

'Only time will give me answers,' she thought. 'We'll see soon enough.'

She wanted to move her fingers over her knees and calves to rub the muscles, but she did not want to risk the movement. 'Don't think about your body, old woman, don't go looking for trouble.' She stretched out her legs as slowly as she dared and gazed out into the night.

She could not see the farm house from here. She knew its direction, but it was too far away and too covered by thicket. The only thing that reminded her of its existence was the baobab tree, its branches stretching across the sky as if to create a safety net in case the moon should fall into its arms.

She used to lie in bed with the boys, looking out onto the tree from their bedroom window. Each night they begged for a different story from her. She had started out with the traditional African myths: the Tale of Superman, the Hyena's Tree and the Anger of the Gods, but the boys wanted her to tell the made-up stories, about the magic that took place in the tree's branches when they all slept – about the creatures and characters that crept from its cracks and immense hollows when darkness fell.

It occurred to her that she had been like Sleeping Beauty all these years, locked in a castle, half asleep, surrounded by a thorny forest, waiting for some magical force to save her. She was too old and cynical to believe in happily-ever-after, but she wondered what it was that she had been waiting for as the seasons piled on top of her. Since the accident, her life had stopped. It was like the spindle had pricked her and she had fallen into a stupor, keeping the farm going, the family going. But after Matthew, nothing had been the same.

She moved her eyes to the horse. He began to relax his head and the soft folds of velvet over his eyes finally began to droop. He lifted his hind leg, shifted his rump and rested the tip of his back hoof on the ground. His chin fell as his head nodded gently.

She waited for fifteen minutes and then she moved, as silently as her old body would allow her, one inch closer to the horse.

The stallion jerked his head up and opened his eyes fully. His ears swivelled and he brought his resting hoof back under his body, square on, but he stayed where he was.

Alma let out a breath. She felt red blood running through her veins. Her mind was alert, no fatigue from the day's walk, and there was no more pain in her knee. 'I'll take it while it lasts,' she thought to herself.

She sat with her back straight, every limb feeling as though it had been pulled out, stretched and warmed up. Right now, she felt like she could mount the horse and ride him to the borders, start a new life for both of them. She wasn't foolish enough to believe this was a permanent state, but she was thankful to whatever magical force was keeping her from time.

It was a full hour until the horse began to arrange himself in a more comfortable position. Even when his head was once more relaxed, his ears stayed forward, twitching at the slightest noise.

When he had been at rest for fifteen minutes, Alma eased towards him another inch. Again, he awoke, but this time he went back to his rest in what Alma thought must have been thirty minutes. Every time the horse eased and rested, she moved an inch closer. The first few times he reacted sharply and then, as if too tired to bother, or realising she presented no danger, allowed her two inches at a time without flinching, just watching from the corner of his eye. Feigning disinterest in her advances.

The night air was cold, sharp, invigorating. She hadn't slept out since she had searched for horses and stray cattle years ago. She used to take a sleeping bag then, food, a pack horse. It made her smile to think that all this time on, here she was, an old woman with just an oilskin jacket, a small bag and nothing to cover herself with.

From the day she arrived at the farm she had preferred to be outdoors. The dark house, the smell of the dogs, it got into her throat, making her breath short and close. She began to search the house, looking for ways to make it bearable to live in.

As she opened a window onto the veranda a gust of air blew in and she wished the whole house could feel like that air. She ran then, from room to room, opening every window she could find – the toilet, the bathroom, the bedrooms, the kitchen, the back door, the front door – until everything was wide open and whatever wisps of curtains were hanging were sucked out, flapping against brickwork. The front door banged open and shut as the wind blew through, but even over the noise of the banging she heard the thin call of another human voice, unmistakable in the bush.

A figure stood at the end of the drive, behind the gate, a black woman with a bundle of blankets.

'What do you want?' Alma called, as she walked towards the gate. Even if the woman was selling something, contact with another human would be welcome.

'Missus. Sorry to disturb. Please. I am looking the job.'

The woman was dusty, her face and hands dry. She had printed fabric tied around her head and in her arms the bundle of blankets. 'Please. I can keep good the house. And my baby, no trouble, very quiet.'

'Your baby?'

Alma looked over the gate and the woman pulled at the blanket to reveal a tiny face, eyes screwed shut, hands curled into fists held close to its cheeks.

'How old is the baby?'

'Five weeks, missus.'

'How did you get here?'

'I walk. Must look the job.'

'Where have you come from?'

'Very far, missus.'

'Your name?'

'Nsousa, missus.'

'Is there a father, Nsousa?'

'No, missus. Just me and the baby.'

Alma looked along the driveway that narrowed into the bush. Heat waves gathered low to the ground where the thorny trees started and she lifted the heavy chain over the gate to let Nsousa in.

Alma's eyes were wide open. That was one thing about age; you were given more time, as though nature recognised encroaching death and compensated by cutting the need for sleep. She wished she'd been given those hours when she was younger, when there was never enough time and her body felt deprived of sleep. What did an old woman want with nineteen wakeful hours a day, with eyes that could not read and limbs that would not run? But here she was, finally, with a purpose for the extra hours.

As they rested, the old woman and the horse, just the scrub and the rocks between them, she described the night's noises to the stallion in her soft female voice. She told him about the bush he was living in, how she would like to show him the limits of the farm way out to the west where the giraffe grazed the thorn trees and where she had once watched a cheetah raise her cub. 'I went out there every day for two months,' she told him. 'Most days I saw them. But the season changed and they moved on. I don't suppose either of them is alive now but I wonder if the bloodline lives on?' She was quiet for a moment. 'Yes, it's a hard place. What with the dangers of the bush, it's almost impossible to raise cubs to maturity. The odds are stacked against them from the start you see, boy.'

Occasionally, the horse answered by way of a soft whinny, which came from his belly, before half-closing his eyes and shifting his weight to another resting hoof. She lay back on the damp earth. 'Bad for my arthritis,' she thought. 'But it's a terminal condition. How much worse can one night outside make it?' If the horse became jittery, one night could extend to two. But she took each moment as it came to her. A training method she had always used.

Night thickened and her vision of the horse was now limited under a waning gibbous moon. To remind herself of what lay ahead, Alma thought back to the day when the chestnut gelding arrived at the farm, running from the trailer, front legs kicking out, head high, rope trailing.

'Think you're a bloody horsewoman?' Jaco had shouted in

his thick accent as he got back into his car. 'Well, here's one that will put an end to your nonsense.'

She sat on the mounting block all night and most of the following day, watching the animal, not daring to approach. It was the first time she had wondered what a horse could have been through to have such fear of humans. It was also the night she began to develop her technique. It was not trickery as the rumours later suggested. It was simple trust and confidence and, for a long time, it had held the farm and the family afloat whilst Kent bought into a stud herd that could not withstand the conditions of farm life.

When Jaco came to collect the gelding a year later, Alma did not have to fight to keep him. The animal stood at the back of his stable, seventeen hands high, flanks muscled, legs strong, ears flat to his head, muzzle pulled back to show a row of yellowing teeth and his newly-shod hooves sparked as they scraped the concrete floor.

She stood at his shoulder, her head not reaching the base of his neck. 'You must take him yourself if you want him.'

From the stable door, Jaco spat at the horse and swore at her.

For years to come he spread rumours about her witchcraft, but it did not matter, the big chestnut gelding was hers to keep. She shut her eyes to close the thought out.

Four hours later and she was as close to the horse as she needed to be. He would be able to smell her from where she was and both the old woman and the horse allowed themselves to relax their muscles and nod their heads.

There were bats in the cave which remained active through the long hours, darting low over their heads, their pungent smell mixing with the night air. The frogs' chorus sounded like a far-off alarm as they called throughout the night.

When light came, she would try to lead the horse to water.

The sky began to fill with the sound of birdsong. She did not feel as though she had slept, but she must have done because she knew she had had the dream again. She is in her bedroom, forty years younger, and she is trying to repack the red suitcase, but every time she opens a drawer to take something out to pack she cannot remember what she is looking for. She goes back to the case, she remembers and she returns to the drawer. What is she here for? Backwards and forwards, treading over the dark floorboards of the room like a spirit of herself, suspended.

There is another dream she still has occasionally, although it did not come to her last night. And it is a strange dream because she did not get married in a traditional wedding gown.

She is in the bush and it is a warm day. She is waiting for Kent to join her. They have to collect something and they must go on foot. She begins the journey alone. He will catch up. Nsousa calls out from the homestead but the voice is distant, carries on the wind and when it reaches her it is too faint. She will find out when she gets home later.

As she walks, the clouds begin to gather overhead, they swirl into great patterns of grey and deep blue and she looks up to see them moving quickly – she has never seen them move so – but she keeps walking forwards because she knows there is something she must collect and it has to be done now, but her dress is heavy around her legs and it is holding her up. As the wind strengthens it blows against her and it slows her so she picks up the hem of her dress to try to move her feet more freely over the stony ground, but the hem seems to be weighed down with stones and she cannot lift it, so she has to lean into the wind and drag the dress every step that she takes and it is not long until the rains start, but she keeps moving forwards and even when they pelt her from above and drive at her from the front, she moves onwards. Although she is hardly moving, she knows that if she stops she will never collect the thing that is waiting for her and so, one inch at a time, she walks into the full force of the storm that is now hitting her from all sides and she can see a typhoon approaching from ahead and it picks up trees with their full roots and boulders that come towards her and she puts her arm up to shelter her face and even though the typhoon races at her she does not give up and then, all of a sudden, she is no longer on the ground but she is ahead in the distance, watching herself. The typhoon passes right by her and she sees herself, remote and small, walking into the remaining winds even though the dress is dragging her down and the veil is whipping around her head. 'You can stop now!' she calls out to herself, but no sound comes out of her mouth. And she has to watch the figure struggling on, dragging the dress, heavy from the rain, torn from the wind, red dirt seeping up into the skirts until it is only a small thing, far away on the horizon.

She was glad she did not have that dream last night.

As the dawn chorus started up, she listened for the rumble of farm trucks or heavy footsteps. Callum's arrival now would undo all her work.

The horse began to pace around as if in an enclosure. He did not want to leave the safety of the cave, but he needed to make decisions about his day. She noted that he kept her in his vision. She was all he knew in the bush now and if she had established a relationship with him he would begin to rely on her for his survival.

She opened her bag, explored the contents, talked softly to herself. The horse watched her. She let her fingers run through the rope, the grain, then she shut the bag. He still watched as she began to rub her arms, circle her ankles and twist her torso.

'We need to get you to water, boy,' she said aloud and with her only thought on the horse and his thirst, she stood up. She stood up too quickly after the stillness of night and her legs buckled under her. She fell to the floor on her knees. No pain, just complete disobedience from her body.

'Well, that's going to be interesting,' she said through laboured breaths. 'We have a long way to go, boy, and I'm an old woman who, as you can see, has a body that might give up at any time.'

She sat back on the floor and continued to rub and circle her joints and eventually there was a sensation like pins and needles which came to her lower legs. As the blood began to flow, sharp stabs of pain began to attack the nerves along her leg and her back, reminding her of yesterday's fall.

A prisoner in own her body, she watched helplessly as the horse trotted away from her, head held high like an impatient lover.

'Dammit, old woman. You've come too far to give in now.' She banged her fist into the ground; a helpless gesture. An image: herself on the floor with the horse, waiting for a rescue party, her husband, Callum, their guns and accusing eyes, finding her, crippled old woman in the bush, hunting her down, as she had hunted for them forty years ago.

'Food. That's what I need,' she said. And wondered if it was a new thing, the way she talked to herself. Nsousa sang and murmured constantly as she went about the house, but Alma was sure she never had.

She pulled a small handful of grain out of her bag and began to chew on the dry chaffs. 'I should have brought some rock cakes and hard cheese,' she thought. 'Some dried figs from the pantry would be good now.' Slowly, her spit worked with the flakes and began to form a porridge-like substance in her mouth. 'Still, this will do. It's only enough energy to get home that I need.' She took some water.

As the oats began to swell and heat in her stomach, she shifted her weight onto her side, bent her knees into her and pushed herself up onto all fours with her hands. She rested, moved into a squat, then pushed up. Shooting pains fired through her legs. It was intense but she was almost upright. She straightened her back. It was done. She began to walk, stiffly, away from the cave.

Black trees were painted on a mustard yellow sky through flecks of pink and blue. Flocks of hadedas swooped from the tall gums, egrets scattered in search of cattle. The wings beat to the rhythm of her heart as she looked into the empty bush. The horse was nowhere to be seen. The rocky ground revealed no tracks.

She began to walk around the back of the cave, along the narrow path that divided it from the koppies. The path used to lead to the water hole. Soft echoes from her footsteps as she hobbled through the fallen stones.

She heard him coming before she saw him. The thud of hooves on soil and rocks and she stood with her back flat to the rock face, leaving what gap she could on the path. As the horse rounded at speed, he saw her and pulled up ten metres in front of her, nostrils flared, breathing hard. His muzzle was dripping with water, it clung in droplets to his whiskers and she smiled as she looked at him.

'So, the waterhole's still there is it, boy?' she said. 'You're becoming a bush horse with instincts.' She praised him in a low whisper and then turned her back on him.

Once again she opened her bag, explored its contents with probing fingers. She had never had to catch a horse in her life. She worked with them until they wanted to come to her and now she was relying on everything she had learnt as she waited for him to respond.

He drew closer, head nodding in interest. She left her back to him waiting, hardly daring to breathe.

And then she felt it.

A nudge in the middle of her back.

Warm, inquisitive.

She took a step forward and waited, grain running through her fingers. Another nudge.

They inched forwards like this for several metres until they were in the open once again. She pulled some grain from the bag, held it in her hand and passed it behind her. Palm open. His lips gently pinched her skin as he drew the grain up. Cupping noises as he chewed on the flakes.

He pushed her more firmly in the back and, as she fed him another mouthful, she took a step back so that she drew parallel with his shoulder. As he chewed, she began to run a hand over his crest in the direction of his coat. Over his shoulder she travelled, stopping at the top of his leg. She let her hand settle there whilst she reached her right arm up to the base of his mane, where the wiry hair met the withers, so that she was standing with her body open to him and her arms wrapped around him. She leant into his warmth. Not moving, breathing softly, murmuring to him. His ears twitched forwards and back and they stood like this for at least ten minutes before Alma drew her arms away and moved ahead, leading.

She felt every joint in her body as she moved. She had trusted in her body yesterday, but today, she didn't know if she should take that risk.

'Keep your mind strong, old woman,' she said. 'Don't trust in strength alone.'

The old woman and the horse walked in step together over the scrub towards the thicket. He could have moved faster but he kept gait with her, missing steps so he didn't overtake her.

She saw them from the corner of her eye before he did; two ground-hornbills, wings flapping and heavy bodies swaying as they came clucking out of the bush, startled by woman and horse. The horse spooked, jumped and leapt to the side. She hadn't realised she had been leaning on the animal and at his sudden departure she fell to the ground. White pain shot through her as she clutched at her knee. She lay winded on her side.

The horse circled her and stamped his feet.

'I'm like a skittle, old boy,' she managed to say as her breath came back to her. 'But I'm made of flesh, not wood.'

The sky above them was endless, cloudless and blue. The vulture, still casting ragged shadows over her in wide circles, was biding his time.

The old lightning tree was to her left and she ran her fingers through the red dirt and let it fall loosely to the ground. There would be no more walking for her now. She had taken too many falls. Her knee was swelling fast and her joints were on fire.

She looked at the horse.

They could wait for whoever might come for them.

Or perhaps there was another way.

A crazy thought.

She looked at his barrel chest. His legs. The hind quarters of carved muscle, his impatient circles, sidesteps skimming the soil.

There was a fork in the tree. If she could get to it, she could pull herself up, use it as a mounting block.

It was a crazy idea.

But it could work.

The horse stayed with her, giving her confidence in her plan, but as she sat upright the blood rushed from her head and flooded her first with cold, then a heat which made darkness pulse through the front of her brain.

Taking her time, she drank the last of her water and took a final piece of bread to chew on.

She sat up again. Took the rope now from her bag. Uncoiled it and began to thread the fine twines together into a halter. The stallion moved closer with interest.

'You've never seen one of these, I bet,' she said to him as she worked her old fingers around the rope. 'People don't do this anymore. Things are easy to buy in the shops now – even here. But it's soft. You'll like it. It'll make you feel like a cowboy's horse. But I'll warn you,' she looked up into his eyes, 'I'm no rodeo rider.'

He turned and stood with his back to her. Tail flicking. 'That's right, boy, you have a think about it.'

He was an incredible beast. He had shown intuition, loyalty, guts, intelligence; everything a horse should possess. He would be a dream to work with and his very presence filled her with emotions she had kept closed for so many years. She hadn't had a partner like this since Mala.

'Mala.' She whispered his name.

'Mala.' She allowed that word to escape her mouth for the first time in forty years and her body warmed at the recall.

It was the name she'd called as a younger woman, uttered over and over, softly as she had trained him, alone, just horse and woman, connected to each other through thought and motion, melding together as one.

Her mind always shut down when Mala came into her head. How could she allow herself the pleasure and pain of his memory? Enough to drive a woman to madness in the lonely bush, with the heat, the cattle, the flies, the endless scrub, the daily callers to her back door requesting medical help, schooling, housing, work, funeral fees, identity cards. And then she'd had her boys to raise and she had made herself get out of bed and deal with every day and every request. And there had been no place for Mala in that new world.

She turned herself once again onto her side. Then shifted onto her front. Once she was on all fours, she tried to push herself to standing, but her legs were no longer strong enough to hold her weight.

'Well, then I'll damn well crawl,' she shouted, startling the horse. And she did. Like an animal, a part of the bush, merging with the surroundings, she shuffled her knees painfully, one ahead of the other through the red dust, shutting out the screeches of pain running through her legs, her arms, her spine.

The horse took small, jerky steps behind her. His companionship kept her moving forwards, towards the tree. Slowly she got closer. Her hands scuffled through the dust; gnarled fingers looked like they could take root as they slid through the dirt.

And then something sharp on her palm. It drew blood. She sucked at it whilst she searched the ground with her eyes. And there, a broken bead, glass maybe. No bigger than her little nail. Faceted, a hole running through the middle. She picked it up and rubbed it. The colour of peacock feathers in the sunshine.

'Damn this dust,' she said as she wiped her eye. 'And what does an old woman like me want with treasures?' she almost shouted.

The horse let out a snort and stamped a hoof on the ground. He arched his crest and shook his neck slightly.

'I'm coming, boy,' she said as she dropped the bead to the ground, not seeing where it fell. She looked only to the lightning tree.

From a kneeling position, she reached up to the lowest fork of the tree, the wood smooth in her hand. She hauled herself up and leant between the fork and the trunk on wavering legs.

She spoke to the horse, keeping him calm, and as he approached she began to work her hands over his face, leant into his wide shoulders, moving her fingers over his muzzle, his cheeks, all the time talking, talking. She slipped the rope gently over his ears, tied it quickly under his jaw, leaving just enough rope for her to hold but not enough for him to trip on if he broke free.

She ran her hands over his legs, his back, his hooves, every part she could reach without using her own legs for support. He stood for her as if trained for war. His trust becoming absolute.

By the time she manoeuvred herself onto the branch and lay herself over his back, he was ready for her. She would usually have circled the horse like this several times before mounting, but her age and condition did not allow for such pleasantries.

Her reflexes took over as she lifted her leg over the stallion's rump and her body propelled itself into an upright position with her legs long around the stallion's body. The horse took a few steps to the side and whinnied low.

Mala. No. She patted his mane, soothed him with words.

Mala. No. She shut her thoughts and reached forwards, picking up the slack of the rope.

Mala.

The last horse she rode was Mala.

Forty-six years ago.

In the paddock, working with Mala. Practicing through the double. Cutting fractions of seconds from the approach. She hears a gun shot. Far away. She turns her head towards the koppies, the caves. She'd had the sense of foreboding since the night before.

Her husband was going to track the wild dogs that had been snatching calves. I'll take the boys. No, she'd said, take the workers. You're trying to raise me three girls, he'd said. And they'd finally agreed he would take Peter and Callum but not Matthew. Not her baby. Even her husband agreed that four was too young for such blood-thirsty activity. Or so he'd said the night before.

She always rode early and returned in time to get the boys up and give them breakfast. Matthew was always asleep when she got back at seven. But today she gets back and they are already gone. Matthew's bed cold, his brown rabbit at right angles on the pillow.

Where are they, Nsousa?

Gone, madam. On foot. Tracking the dogs.

And Matthew?

Gone with them, madam. Mister insisted good for him.

She runs out onto the veranda. Around the house. They'd left early. No sign of them. She calls but there's no reply. Her voice sounds empty to her. Hunting is a whole day's sport. Matthew will be hungry, thirsty, hot. He won't keep up. Stupid man. He has no idea of children. He'll get annoyed with Matthew. He's just a baby. My baby. He has no right…

She takes the Land Rover to see which way they've gone.

There are no clues. The gears stick, she lets the clutch out. It stalls, she is angry and floods the engine and has to walk back along the track to the house.

Nsousa brings coffee. I can't drink it, Nsousa. I'm going out. She straps her half-chaps onto her calves and strides into the stable block.

Mala waits calmly for her. For his morning routine. Chestnut coat gleaming russet. She feels his hot breath on her cheeks as he greets her. Velvet muzzle brushes her arm. She always tacks him up herself. And he towers over her as they stand side by side in the paddock.

We'll work the double today. Don't want you getting lazy on me.

She tightens his girth, pulls his legs forward to release trapped skin. Pretends to brush his mane all to one side and rests her arms around him, momentarily feeling his warmth and strength, smelling the hay scent trapped in his coat. Wishing her arms could be wrapped around her baby boy and that she could be smelling his scalp, toasty hair.

She rides him hard, drops the crop, shifts her weight to the side, reaches to the ground and picks it up, righting herself immediately, kicking the animal into a gallop. Horse and rider one as they change legs mid-air, five strides out and shorten for the jump. She lifts her seat right out of the saddle, her breast over his head, all weight off his back as he soars over the striped white and red bars.

She cries exhilaration into the air. Mala shakes his head and squeals. They will win this weekend. She knows she has the best horse. Mala too knows he is the best.

Then she hears it through her own cries. The gunshot. Clear. Distant. The foreboding clutches at her chest.

She pushes Mala on and they jump the gate. She doesn't hesitate as she pushes him on into the bush. He picks up on her panic. Over the track, through the gorse, in between the acacia. The enormous horse speeding through the bush like a kudu on the run. She soon sees the koppies in the distance. She's shouting now, pushing Mala on. He lathers, she can hardly breathe.

Please God.

They are walking towards her. Three figures. There should be four. As she draws closer, she sees her husband carrying the smallest.

Callum is crying. Snot running into his lips.

I'm sorry, Mummy, he is saying as she jumps down from Mala.

Matthew has been shot. His eyes closed. He is breathing. She doesn't ask. She jumps back onto her horse.

Give me my boy.

Her husband hands him up silently.

She closes him into her jacket. Holds him tightly to her with one arm. She doesn't stop to kiss him before she pushes Mala into a gallop.

They take the quickest road home; the track. The ground is dry. Hard. Deeply rutted.

They are flying over the bush, too fast to think. He stumbles; she pulls him up through the reins. His head jerks; she pushes him on. He falls. A crack she has never heard before. Could never have imagined.

They all fall to the ground; she rolls clear with Matthew.

The horse is screaming. His neck twisting in the red dirt, trying to raise himself.

The bottom half of his front leg, trapped in a hole. Snapped in two. White bone splintering at the knee.

His eyes roll, searching for hers. He finds her and screams into the hot air. He's still for the second that he looks into her eyes. His trust in his mistress absolute. Even now, waiting for her direction, his trust is absolute.

Her boy dying in her arms. She doesn't know what sound

she makes as she turns her back on Mala and runs towards the house. She doesn't stop as she runs away from his screams and not for one moment do they stop or quieten in her mind. She reaches the door.

Nsousa is there.

I have called the doctor.

Get blankets, Nsousa!

She lays him on the kitchen table. His chest scarlet.

She rips his tiny sweater away from his body, tries to open his eyes. Feels for a pulse. Gives him mouth-to-mouth. Her baby child lies dead in her arms.

Her hair wild from the blood, her clothes wet through and scarlet, she turns to the door. She might be screaming.

She runs back into the bush, knows exactly the path to take. Her breath comes strong and her heart beats with her life.

Her husband is standing away from Mala. Unable to look at any of them. Shotgun in his hand.

The horse has a single bullet through his head, a dark circle in the wide area between his brown eyes where the chestnut infuses with a blaze of white.

She falls to the floor and now she hears herself. A long screech. High-pitched, animalistic. The noise Mala had made as she left him dying alone in the bush. She scratches at the dirt with her hands. Runs them through her hair, sobbing. A woman driven mad with grief.

Take the boys home, she shouts.

Her husband hesitates.

TAKE THEM!

They begin to walk away from her and she stands silently watching their backs.

She turns to Mala. His broken body lying in the dirt. His chestnut pelt stained with the sweat and the dirt and the blood.

She will bring him home. She moves the splintered knee out of the hole. She ungirths his saddle and throws it to the side. She tries to roll him onto the level surface. She is a strong woman; she can do this. She rolls him, drags him, pushes him, gets her feet under his ribs. She needs to get him home. She is lost to herself and this task.

When she comes round, she is lying on the floor next to Mala, knee bent under her. A vulture circling overhead, expectant with the smell of death. There is no pain in her legs and there is no feeling. She rests her head on him.

She knows she cannot move and will have to wait.

Something will happen soon enough.

The stallion moved off voluntarily. Like he could no longer stand still with the new weight on his back. As Alma jolted forward, she felt the fatigue of her memories weighing on both her and the horse.

'Matamba,' she said out loud. 'A noble name for a noble horse.' To be sitting astride him, loosely holding the rope, this powerful beast. It was a thing that brought tears to her eyes.

The horse carried Alma along the track that would lead them straight to the farm. His legs, sure under them, made no more skittish movements. His hooves fell on the soil.

Thud-thud, thud-thud, thud-thud.

The journey had tired her and she allowed herself to be rocked in the mist of chestnut which escaped from his flesh. Her hands fell involuntarily to his mane to steady herself and she grasped wisps of hair that strayed at the base of his withers. The hair, wiry and strong between her fingers, chaffed at her old skin and, for a while, it was enough to keep her eyes from drooping. With each step the horse took, the house and paddocks drew nearer. But the rocking was so comfortable that time began to slide until she jerked her head up suddenly to find the house right in front of her. She opened her old eyes wide in the sunlight. Her home was detailed in a way that she had never seen before. Lit up in the bright sun, so bright she had to shield her eyes against it. The white-washed walls, the cement veranda that wrapped along the back, the jacaranda showing purple flowers on every branch, the aloe spikes pointing skywards, a single trail of smoke over the workers' dorp.

And above the stables, tiny birds gathering in great flocks, rising in waves of beating wings then descending over the roof of the empty stables before scattering over the trees and regrouping together against the bright white sky. They were making an almighty noise so that Alma had to put her hands to her ears suddenly.

She brought her eyes to rest on the ménage and she saw herself, leather chaps strapped to her legs, one horse at the block ready to mount, another tacked up and gazing at her from his stall.

She calls to the waiting horse as she puts her foot in the stirrup. 'You'll get your turn next. Don't get sentimental on me; you have to go home next week.' He nods his head upwards in response; his ears twitch forwards then back.

All this she does whilst pretending to herself that she is not waiting for Kent. She schools the horse, takes him over several fences, drives him forward into the bit, makes him work his neck, build his muscle and learn control. This one is too rangy. If he doesn't make the grade, his owners will lose interest and horses that don't make the grade have uncertain futures.

Her eyes always glancing to the track for signs. Dust hovering over the road, the call of a loerie, a distant shout or engine noise. All afternoon she works like this, dragging her mind back to her task, all the time the words she has rehearsed go through her head in disjointed lines like a play performed in scattered acts.

She had the chance once, and she had allowed it to slip away with a bright smile and a brave face. The way a nice girl is supposed to. Maybe it is the sun that has hardened her, perhaps the hours of solitude, but she is not going to lose another opportunity. When Kent comes home, she has a speech prepared and she is going to deliver it.

The night is thick when he finally arrives. She hears the engine rattle to a halt, the door slam, the workers' feet fall heavily along the path to the dorp.

She gets out of bed, puts on her dressing gown and walks barefoot along the cold passage to the entrance.

He is surprised to see her up at this hour and drops his pack to the ground.

'I'll make tea,' she offers. The tea will give them something to do.

'Any success?' She pokes the fire with an iron whilst he sits in a kitchen chair, his feet apart, his elbows on his knees.

'Truck broke down two hours from Mesassa. Put us back three days. Bloody locals don't know what they're doing with machinery. I should've taken Clive.'

'So you didn't buy any stock?'

'We didn't even get to the sale.' He scrapes the grain of the table with a fingernail.

She puts the kettle on the hot plate and gathers cups, sugar, milk, arranging them in a semi-circle in front of him. Her mouth is dry and she runs her tongue over her front teeth.

When she has poured the tea she sits opposite him. His restlessness is palpable, but opportunities do not present themselves: they have to be made.

She opens her mouth to speak, hardly knowing which line she will use first. The loneliness, the need to make peace with her family, disillusionment with Africa, the savings she has never told him about, they all crowd into her mouth at once for her to pick at. She is ready to talk now; she will start with the soft option – her parents. But her chest tightens and it is all she can do to hold down her tea. She feels her bread-and-cheese supper move in her stomach and rise to burn her throat and she can hardly believe she is being governed by nerves at this stage. She is so close.

'You okay? You look pale.' He half gets up from his chair to go to her, but she runs from the kitchen and vomits on the bathroom floor, her moment slipping into a chasm that will not open up for her again.

A child seals fate. Even before her body swells, she knows she must accept the life which she is now bound to in the most physical way.

Right now, the house looks so beautiful, it seems hard to imagine a time when she would have wanted to escape it. Surely this is one of the splendid places on earth. A wild and remote place where a mind can wander as far as the feet without disturbance. A sky above, so open and clear that eternity seems within reach.

She is looking forward to getting home. She wants to feel the grain of the oak on her kitchen table, see the feathered cracks on her china cup as she drinks hot rooibos and she wants to listen to the cicadas tonight as she sits on her porch chair, watching the full moon rise over the baobab tree, making its silent journey across the night sky, disappearing behind the marula until it comes to its final resting place above the orange haze of the early-morning koppies where it will wait for a watery sun to push it into opaque obscurity, high in the dawn sky.

The rhythm of the horse slowly rocks her.

Thud-thud, thud-thud, thud-thud.

The stallion keeps a steady head and an easy gait.

Thud-thud, thud-thud, thud-thud.

Alma wants to stay awake, but her eyes are so heavy, and the stallion's movements are so comforting.

Thud-thud, thud-thud, thud-thud.

Her eyes are so heavy and her body feels so limp that she allows herself to slump forward onto the horse, just for a moment, until she has rested and is able to sit up again.

Her arms flop loosely around his neck and she feels the silk of his coat on her cheek, but he holds his head steady and keeps an easy gait, taking her shift in weight without complaint.

As the truck approaches, the stallion becomes wary. His eyes move towards the vehicle, but it slows on approach and stops a way off.

A man climbs out, in his hand a soft rope, coiled the way his mother has shown him.

Slowly, allowing the horse enough space at each step, he draws nearer, until man and horse regard each other at close range.

The man sees he will not need the rope he has been preparing all afternoon and his eyes fill as he sees the old woman folded over the stallion's withers.

He goes gently to the horse, making no attempt to snare it, and they walk side by side, along the farm track towards the house and to the stables.

As the man walks in time with the horse, he notices the silence all around them. The noon heat has stilled the birds, the dogs have all sought shade for the afternoon, and with the heat comes a feeling of emptiness, of futility.

There is nothing more he can do now and he knows that the time for him to move on will come, perhaps sooner than he is ready for.

But for now, he walks. He walks in time with the horse and he thinks of the old woman.

The smell of the hot soil is heavy in the air and a light wind begins to blow in from the east.

WHO HAS TO MAKE THESE DECISIONS?

Mama, it's dark.

I know, baby.

I'm scared.

I know.

I hold her hand in mine. It is a small hand. And mine is big, which means that I am in charge. Big hand, small hand. Big person, small person. I am responsible. For everything. She is right, it is dark inside. I have never seen such darkness. I know there are others inside but I cannot see them. And there is the smell. So strong, I am sure we will be sick, or worse. If the worst comes, I do have the tablets. But only eight. They are in my pocket. I will not lose them. They would not be enough to even put me to sleep, but her, perhaps they could help her. Would I do that? I have thought about it. If it becomes too much, if something happens and we cannot bear it, then I would give them to her. But to put them in my hand and push them into her throat. I don't know. Who has to make these decisions?

Mama?

We are the last. The last of a slow line of people who were so eager at the start of our journey, but now tired, not sure, not expecting – this. They moved slowly. Up the ladder, one at a time. Hurry, we were told. Hurry, we have to go. One rung, two rungs, three, four, five. Sixteen, I counted. Sixteen steps. And how many people? Yes, I counted them too. Forty-eight.

Forty-six are in. They have all made their decision.

Hurry, we must go, says the voice from below. The ladder shakes underneath us. As the ground has shaken beneath us so many times before. The ground that shook so much it filled us with its shaking so that we thought it would never stop.

I made the decision to go because of her. For myself, perhaps I would not have bothered. What is my life? But her life; that is something. That is worth something.

My body aches with the effort of getting us here, but standing at the mouth of the tank makes me think. If her life is so precious, why risk it? What is the bigger risk – this or that? That or this?

I have to decide. The smell is overwhelming and we are not even inside yet. How bad will it be? She is so small. How much can she stand?

Who has to make these decisions? Have we gone too far to get back? Could we stay here? What if I say no? I have never been very good at saying no. It is not in our culture for women to say no.

It is not in our culture for women to say very much. We must even act like we are not thinking. There is a special expression we learn from our mothers. The face, smooth. The eyes, lowered. Expression blank. Nothing. We do not hear. We do not speak. We do not see. I have never cared for my own safety and, as I grew older, I thought, yes, I could do something. I could make a stand, draw attention. Others had done it. I could get onto social media, get into a newspaper in another country. But too soon it was too late. Because I had created another life. And I wasn't sure if it was the creation of that other life that gave me the strength or whether it was the creation of that other life that held me back.

Who has to think about these things?

She looks like me. A particular brown to the eye that is mine, high forehead, wide cheeks. A beautiful girl. She has your beauty, my husband said when he first saw her. But I was not so happy. For a woman to be beautiful is for a woman to be noticed. And where we come from, it is not good for a woman to be noticed. A blessing or a curse? Who can tell? Where have my looks got me?

My looks have got us here. I did not want my daughter's looks to have to do the same for her. And in a new place? Who could say that place would be better? I have been told so many times – if we could get to Great Britain there would be help. They would not let a mother and child starve. Or be cold, or afraid, or sick. There is a welfare state that will provide for all – even people like us. It is hard to imagine a country like that. I will not believe it until I see it. If we could get there, we would be safe. That is what I have learnt from the news I have been allowed to see, the conversations I have been allowed to hear, the papers I have been able to read. The women talk when no one is watching. And all the little things we see, we hear, we read, we learn, together we have something. Tiny moments. So slight that no one would know. Looks, notes, a conversation behind a closed door – but all of this is punishable.

Punish me. That is how I feel. Punish me because I don't care. I don't believe in your rules. I don't believe. I never believed. But now there is another life. Another life I have made. And I must keep that life safe. I must give my life to save that life. And so, now, I do care. I must care.

Mama?

Yes, darling?

She looks at me. Brown of the eyes that is mine, the curve of the lip, the brow. My face in another. My child.

Yes, darling?

Do we have to go back?

Back?

Back, she says. There.

I feel a tightening of her hand in mine, small hand, big hand. My hand, her hand. My child, her mother. She said back. There. She did not say back home. She did not say, back to the father who left us to defend a way of life we did not believe in. She did not say, back to the school that refused to give her a proper education. She did not say, back to the grave of my parents who would have given anything to see us leave the borders of this country.

She did not say those things. She said, Do we have to go back. There?

The stench is overwhelming and I check my pocket and I still have the tablets and I look down at the ground to the small bag we are not allowed to bring and I hold her hand in my hand.

No, I say to her. We do not have to go back. There.

We inch forward into the darkness. Soft hands reach out to guide us. We sit and we wait as the hatch closes and the last shaft of light leaves us. My life is nothing. I would give it up in a second. But that is not an option anymore.

My life is nothing. But hers, that is something. Who has to make these decisions? A mother has to make these decisions. I put my lips to her ear.

Don't be afraid, I whisper. There is nothing to be afraid of anymore. Did I tell you the story about the lady who lived with her daughter in a little house on the edge of the city? Did I tell you how she took her daughter to school every morning on a bicycle, then on the way home she bought fresh bread and milk and then every day she collected her daughter from school and in the evenings they would sit together and the daughter would tell her mother of all the wonderful things she had learnt?

Tell me again, Mama, my daughter says, and I feel her yawn against my body.

Yes, I will tell you again, I say. But only a little bit now. Because, soon enough, you will see it all for yourself.

The smell of the petrol is not so bad now that we are inside.

If her life matters, then my life matters. And her life matters so much that I will get us to wherever we need to be. It is the creation of that other life that has given me strength. I have always known it. But now, on this journey, in this darkness, with my arms around her, I know it for sure.

THE YOUNGEST CHILD

The youngest child hangs like a spectre over the whole family. She is, to the mother, more present than her surviving children. Collected things in a small leather case to be shown to future generations. A pair of silken ballet shoes, a wooden hairbrush with auburn strands still woven through the bristles, pencil sketches, incomplete schoolbooks, *A Tale of Two Cities;* hardback turning soft with the ripening of age.

From the other children some letters, postcards, a door closed on a childhood bedroom, no things. Because their things are infinite. There will always be more of them. Too much of them cluttering the space that the missing child fills.

Such silent reverence when her name is uttered. A quiet respect that is afforded to no other in the family. Only the mother feels this pain. It is for no one else. Why, no one else in the family is a mother! They did not carry her and bring her into the world and feed her at their breast! They cannot know.

And gradually, over time, it does become only her tragedy. Everyone else moves on. Her children leave home, as she knew they would, and they go far, as she knew they would, and then her husband also leaves her and after all that has passed, after all these years, she has been proved right. It is only a mother that can bear this pain and she alone. That is a pain which never leaves and never dulls and when her mind has gone and she herself is ready to go, there is only one tendril of thought left amongst the debris of dementia and old age.

Will I see Her? Will She be waiting? Have I been true enough to have this one, final reward?

BREAD

Sophie saw the girl approach the car in front. She hated seeing children beg.

She kept her hands at ten-to-two on the wheel and her eyes on the mountains ahead. The slopes were shadowy and under a dense thicket of trees, but the tops were bright where the sun fell. The sky was blue and a single cloud travelled slowly along the ridge from left to right.

No, sorry. That was always her response. She thinned her lips when she said it and shook her head to the side. She *was* sorry, but what difference could a rand or two make to anyone's life?

A big smile showing white teeth. Funny Money?

No, sorry.

A brisk walk past her car – a show of goods at her window like it was a shop front. Township pictures?

No, sorry.

A string bag held overhead. Avocados?

No, sorry.

An open plastic bag that she was sure would end up in a ditch later today, filled with newspapers, empty Vida cups, chocolate wrappers. Any rubbish?

Not today.

And then the girl. Hands held out. Large brown eyes. Unusually intense. She bounced up and down as she looked into the car. As if she needed the toilet.

Any change? The voice was dulled through the glass of the window. Sophie never opened the window. It was grotesque the way it slid down to reveal a pair of hands poised in prayer, asking, begging.

Any change?

No, sorry.

Sophie looked to the mountains. The cloud had passed by but she could feel the girl, still there.

Please help me! I need money for bread!

Sophie turned and saw the girl's fingers almost touching the glass, the palms of her hands white and dry, her body moving up and down.

Please! There is nothing to eat in the house. I have nothing. Nobreadnothing! Anything you can give me. Please! The girl bounced more and she looked with large eyes into the car.

It was the tone, no, the words, no, the image. The girl moving up and down, the child with no food in her home, the empty cupboards – it was all those things, all at once. Sophie never broke her rules. Break them once and things got too confusing, too overwhelming.

Please! the girl said. Had she seen Sophie waiver? The lights changed but the girl remained.

I have nothing! I need to eat! One rand. Anything! Her voice high and urgent.

Sophie took the purse from her bag on the passenger seat and quickly opened it. The car in front was already moving. There was a twenty-rand note and some change. She spilled the change onto her hand, slid the window down and rolled the change onto the girl's hands without touching the dry palms. She accelerated and heard the voice more clearly without the glass between them.

Bless you, sister.

Sophie was shaking. The girl's urgency had affected her. Was she really going to buy bread or was it a well-honed act?

Perhaps she wanted money for fast food, Mr Price clothes, electronics, the cinema. Did that small child really go home to empty cupboards? She was shaking. The girl's urgency had affected her and she could not stop thinking about it all the way to town.

As Sophie drove home later, she looked for the girl at the junction. She slowed, almost expecting to see her collecting money from every car – an act that couldn't be refused – but the girl was not there.

Funny Money, township pictures, late-edition Argus, flowers bigger than the man selling them. The girl was not there.

Sophie drove along the highway and she thought of those words, Bless you, sister. It had affected her. She would tell her husband later. But when he got back, he had some news of his own and Sophie forgot all about it.

★★★

Sisi looked in her hand at the change. Maybe ten rand but she did not count it. She put it in her pocket and slid it into the piece of cloth she kept there. She looked up at the mountains. The light had moved far right and she knew it was time to go.

She walked back along the main road, passing beggars and bead sellers, and she turned down past the garage. It was very hot. Better hot than cold, but it was a long walk and she was thirsty. She would have to wait.

She stopped one block before she got to the taxi and turned the corner by the Chinese clothing shop. It was quiet at the back of the shop and she stood in the doorway – amongst the packing crates, the rubbish and the things nobody wanted to buy – and she counted her fare from five-, ten- and twenty-cent pieces. She held the money in one hand whilst she folded the rest back into the cloth and put it in her pocket. She would not look at the taxi driver when she gave it to him. If she gave him a chance, he would throw her off with her small change, and tell her to get silvers or not come at all. When she gave it to him, she would make sure she dropped it quickly in his hand and walk straight to the back of the bus.

Music played in the taxi and nobody spoke over the driver's singing as they waited at the lights. There were no beggars at the lights, no spare change here. They took the highway out of town and Sisi was glad she had a seat today.

When the taxi stopped it was getting dark. There was no more tarmac road and when she got to the shop there was no welcome for Sisi.

Out! the woman said.

Sisi showed the woman six rand coins, silver in her palm.

What do you want?

Any stale bread?

No. Only full price. Half a loaf with that.

Sisi held the money out as the woman halved the bread and put it into an old Blue Ribbon packet. She could see behind the woman as she moved. Bar One, Tex, Aero, Dairy Milk, Time Out, KitKat, Jungle Bar, Coke, Fanta, Lays chips, peanuts, bananas, oranges, mangoes, tomatoes, meat pies.

She paid for the bread and walked home along the track.

When she got there she pushed open the door. She stood inside, opened the bag and took two slices from the top. She ate the bread and as she ate she smelled the coins on her hands. She ate quickly then put her cup into the bucket and drank. The water and the bread bloated her stomach.

She sat on her blanket and counted the slices. Eight left. She took three more out and put them under her pillow. The rest, she left in the bag on the crate by the door. When her father got home it would be better if there was something for him to eat.

She lay down and felt the bread under her pillow. She should wait until morning to eat another slice, but she did not know if she could wait that long.

MOTHER

We live in an old chaos of the sun,
Or old dependency of day and night,
Or island solitude, unsponsored, free,
Of that wide water, inescapable.
Deer walk upon our mountains, and the quail
Whistle about us their spontaneous cries;
Sweet berries ripen in the wilderness;
And, in isolation of the sky,
At evening, casual flocks of pigeons make
Ambiguous undulations as they sink,
Downward to darkness, on extended wings.

Sunday Morning, Wallace Stevens

His foot is the last thing she sees of him. Size eight, Woolworths, a brown leather shoe. Buy the ones with Spiderman on the front, she said. No Mummy, he said, I like these ones. He is not a boy who likes to run outside. He is not a boy who wants to hang from monkey bars and jump from trees and bump into things on a bicycle. He is a boy who likes the company of his mother. He is a boy who likes to read and to help cook dinner. But as she sees his foot disappear from sight and hears the light thump of small bones on dense turf, she wishes she had prepared him better for the journey he now faces, alone.

When he stands up, he must look north. If he looks north, he will at least start on the right path. She closes her eyes. She must concentrate. Concentrate, but not sleep. She must not sleep. She wonders if it is strange that the first thing she should see when she closes her eyes is Guru Shara. Long white robes against a backdrop of green Catskill Mountains, a beard of light wispy hair stroking his chest, his arms spread wide.

You must look beyond sight itself. She can hear his voice clearly in her head, warm, deep, like a double bass being played in an underground cave. Close your eyes and centre your thoughts, he said. She remembers closing her eyes and seeing only the darkness that lay behind her own eyelids, veins of sunlight visible to her through the flesh.

She imagines her son standing up on the grassy patch under the window, rubbing the back of his neck the way he does when he feels nervous, then she sees him pull softly on the lobe of his ear for a moment. He sucked his thumb until he was nearly three and even now, whenever he is unsure, she notices the tip of his thumb held lightly in his mouth. You'll get bunny teeth, she used to warn him. He would snatch his thumb away. I don't want bunny teeth. The little worry line would appear between his eyes, on the bridge of his nose, then he would ask her for the rest of the day, Are they sticking out? I don't want bunny teeth. Do I have bunny teeth? Until she said, Smile like this, show me. And then, No, definitely no bunny teeth. In fact, you have quite the whitest and straightest teeth I have ever seen. Only then, when she had paid him the highest compliment, would he relax.

She holds his image in her mind. She allows her senses to feel him. The toast and chalk smell of him, the taste of his blood when she sucked his finger. It's okay Mummy, he said, it's just a cut. They had been away from the house, to the northern-most point of the farm, where the mountain water met the valley floor and he pulled hard on a piece of razor fence sticking up from the ground. The wire was rusty, wet, and as she sucked the pad of his finger, she felt his blood, hot on her tongue, like bitter chocolate. Now we're blood brothers, he giggled and she felt the pull at the back of her throat when she swallowed. Your blood is made from my blood, she said. I'm just claiming a little of it back.

When she was sure it was clean, they continued their walk through the vines. She stopped and reached out to nip a grape from the bunch. She wanted to wipe away the velvety resin coating and see the flesh shine through. It was like wiping the window of an old shop to see what treasures were hidden inside. The grape was full and firm in her fingers, but the taste was still acidic, the skin too thick. It would not be long though, perhaps another week and they would be ready for the first harvest. She felt a light movement in the base of her stomach. Guru had said the only way to conquer fear was to face it. Face it and you can do it; that was step one of his book. What had her mother said? British women have backbone, Victoria. They prop up society. Yes, her mother had said that a lot.

Finn reached up and took her hand.

You don't have to hold my hand, she said.

I want to, he said as he looked ahead at the dusty track they were following.

I won't disappear into a puff of smoke, she said.

OK, he said.

And then the air suddenly felt very close. She stopped to take off her neck-scarf. Let's sit a moment, sweetheart, she said, and they sat on the rough earth, sharp stones digging through trousers, into flesh, and looked out onto the rows of grapes. There were vines planted ahead of them as far as she could see. They looked like corn-rows on an African woman's head. They weaved over the field in front of them, onto the foothills and folded into the valley, where there were more vines that only stopped at the rocky outcrops. To the north-eastern mountains were sauvignon blanc grapes, planted there for the sandstone and shale terrain which should give the grapes a crisp freshness. In front of her, over the river and beyond the workers' compound, were shiraz grapes.

She had never liked shiraz before coming to South Africa, a bloody and dark wine, complex in the mouth with a slightly smoky aftertaste, but after drinking it a few times, it seemed to represent the way she felt about this country. The first time she tried a local shiraz she was being polite, the same way she had been with her father. Wine was something a young lady was supposed to know about. He had taught her regions, terroirs, varieties, the aroma, the correct glass to drink from. He liked a dry French Chablis and therefore so did she. For her father, knowing about wine was as important as knowing how to hold a knife and fork correctly; it was social etiquette.

As she held the glass in her hands, she swirled the ruby fluid and smelled it. She was in a new place, with new people. Make friends, Owen had told her before they came out. We want a good crowd to invite to all the parties we'll be throwing. I want us to be the toast of Cape Town. She looked at Owen, standing by the marble statue in the reception room and she could catch words from a story she had heard him tell before about a rowing trip he had taken with a television actor on Central Park Lake and how they had to be rescued by two teenage boys on a boat because they had lost their paddle. The woman he was talking to was laughing as the story went on. Owen was better at making friends than she was.

It's from a local vineyard, her host said. I love it; tell me what you think. She prepared her face, prepared herself to say something positive, but she was surprised to find the wine was full, round and vanilla-inflected with ripe berries and wood. It was still complex, still interesting, yet so drinkable. Like a precious rock, it was multi-faceted and, like a precious rock, as she held the wine in her mouth then swallowed it, she began to imagine that there was something she had not felt before and she wanted to reach inside herself, dig it up and examine it.

She saw a smile on her host's face. You like it then? he asked.

She thought for a moment, took another mouthful. Yes, she said. I do.

She had not really thought about work since leaving New York, but after tasting that wine and seeing Owen so comfortable in his new role, an idea began inside her and grew over the weeks that followed.

She began to investigate the shiraz market in the Western Cape. She bought every shiraz that was recommended to her by sommeliers, wine books, vintners and bottle shops and she began to plan her days around trips to wine farms, travelling methodically by region, and talked for long afternoons with wine tasters and cellar staff, always a large round glass of shiraz in her hand.

When she got home, she would line them up, try them blindly and begin to piece together the contents of each. The act of pouring the deep, tannin-inflected wine was something cathartic to her. She held the tilted glass to her nose, inhaled the spicy fruits, let them swirl in her mouth before she felt the dryness pucker the middle of her tongue. She waited for the smoky aftertaste that singed the base of her throat and the way it heated her gullet as it coursed into her stomach. Each time she savoured the wine, she engaged with something about herself that she could not yet identify. The wine made her feel this land was expectant in the way that England and America no longer were. It was hard to find a way in those places, everything had been done before. But South Africa was like she imagined the Wild West had been. There was everything to do and everything to try.

As her eyes rested on the vines ahead of her, she removed her hat and fanned her face and neck with it. She directed the air to Finn who sat quietly beside her. Most boys of his age would fidget and moan. Aren't you hot? she asked him. A bit, he said. It's so hot, she said. What must it be today? Over thirty? Yes, he said. Definitely over thirty. February was the hottest time of year. It made working conditions unbearable, but it provided the heat needed for the final ripening. The leaves withered on the vines, no longer plump and green as they had been a couple of months ago. She wanted to water them so desperately, but they had to be parched to squeeze the last drops of sweetness from them. It was cruel to watch the drooping and wilting leaves turn crispy in the sun, but the browner they turned, the closer they got to harvest. The sweat at the back of her neck was cold. She heard the deep base-notes of Guru's voice: Push your boundaries, come back stronger. She heard her father's voice talking to her mother whilst she listened at the top of the stairs: You must make more time for Victoria, she's becoming wishy-washy. Why don't *you* make time for her? her mother asked. Me? said her father. With all the travel I do? And what about *my* commitments? her mother almost shouted. There was silence for a moment then her mother said, Perhaps boarding school is the best thing for her after all.

You don't mind if I have a quick cigarette, do you? she asked Finn. I'm feeling a bit light-headed. She took out a packet of Marlboro from the top pocket of her shirt and flipped open her Zippo – a tiny piece of her physical past that she had brought with her. Nice lighter, someone had once observed. She can remember shutting it and looking at it. Thanks. I guess that's my way of asking you to light a cigarette for me, he'd said. She had done as he asked and put the lighter back into her bag. So, you live here then or are you just visiting, with that accent? He was a few inches taller than her and had blond hair, about her age and was wearing faded denims and a smart pink shirt. She had heard the term preppy. That was it; he was preppy in a fresh, clean, handsome way. The sort of man she would like to wake up and see next to her in bed. But it ended the way all her encounters ended, with men and women alike. She knew she put up barriers, that was what the university psychologist's report had said: Victoria puts up barriers in social situations. Wishy-washy nonsense, her father had said.

She lit her cigarette and snapped the Zippo shut then blew the first line of smoke straight up towards the watery moon, which still hung low over the mountains like a piece of tracing paper, cut out and stuck onto a painted-blue background.

Yes, I do mind, Finn said. Because you *might* disappear in a puff of smoke one day.

When he said that, she ground the un-smoked cigarette under the toe of her boot and she put her arm around him, then kissed him on the top of his head. His short thick hair prodded at her lips.

Those hairs pressed into her lips, the smell of marshmallow shampoo, the feel of the soft fleshy pads of his fingers, the bitter chocolate taste of his blood, the warmth of the sun on his clothes as she laid her arm over him, the folds of the brushed cotton T-shirt he wore. She lets these thoughts rise to the top of her head and settle. She tries to still her mind and concentrate only on her son.

She could not remember what she had been expecting to see the first time she drove out to the farm. Apart from a photo and a brief outline of the property, there had been little information on it. She knew it had been on the market for two years, not lived in for nearly five, and it had been farmed by an Afrikaans farmer and his wife. But that was all the information available. The photo was a small image cut out and stuck onto an estate-agent's sheet, a tatty piece of paper, almost like the agent had given up trying to sell it. There was something about the lack of care that made her feel sorry for the farm; perhaps it just needed someone to believe in it. The day after receiving the information, she was on the road, making the two-hour trip out of town.

Life will guide you, let it take your hand. That had been the language of the ashram, the place where she had hoped to find the missing links within herself. But all the time she was there she kept wondering if it was possible to change who she was so late in her life. Her heritage felt like an imprint, no matter how far away from it she got.

She could see the name plate on the wall as she approached. Heimat was written in tarnished bronze letters on the entrance wall, the whitewash now yellowing and cracked. Young, leafless trees bordered the driveway and weeds grew around them, clinging to the narrow trunks. As she rounded the corner, she saw the house for the first time. A long, one-storey building in traditional Cape Dutch architecture, wrap around verandas staggered with pillars and a high gabled entrance with 1872 inscribed in florid lettering above the door.

As she entered, she was surrounded by the smell of the thatch – a straw field being mown on a hot day – and her boots crunched over the gritty red flagstones. The house was cool, dark – small windows to keep out the heat of summer and the winds of winter, the agent explained without prompting.

As she walked through the old house, it felt as if someone had gone out one morning and never returned. On the entrance table, a vase of dried flowers coated in dust; as the entrance hall opened to the dining room, she could see the chair cushions were still dented as though someone had just got up from the table. On the table, a pillar candle in a wrought iron holder with a brittle, sooty wick at the top and wax drips suspended on its shaft. To the right, the kitchen, brighter with larger windows, plates still on the drainer, crockery in the dresser, a mat on the floor where someone had stood while washing up. The furnishings are included, the agent noted as she ticked something off on her sheet of paper.

They walked out of the kitchen, through stable doors onto the back veranda, the agent's shoes sharp and intruding, her own, soft and silent. From here, the whole of the farm unfolded. Pink and white roses surrounded the veranda. Beyond, a garden, spiky weeds amongst soft grasses. Farther still, the dam, grass banks all around, reeds tangled with lilies, willows overhanging the water with small baskets swaying from thin switches. Flashes of feathers in the sunlight, yellow, red, white. Beyond the dam, the river and beyond the river, the valley floor which eventually folded into the distant mountains.

The valley unravelled like a rug and the mountains surrounded the farm's borders. The house stood like a stage in a wild and long-forgotten amphitheatre and she could not help wondering if the performance had already begun or if it was long over.

As she stood on the veranda with the sun on her shoulders and the gentle sounds of the idle farm around her, she began to feel that she had allowed life to guide her enough already. Perhaps it was the desire to make something out of what she had been given or perhaps it was more basic than that. Perhaps it was the new life growing quietly inside her that was forcing her to make a home, to leave a legacy.

On the drive home she pulled the car over on the pass to rest. As she waited, she watched a baboon troop. A baby clung to its mother's back; its head buried in her fur as she picked seeds from the grass verge. A large male sat on his haunches in the middle of the road, his head high and enquiring as though defying the onslaught of traffic. Younger baboons ran into the road to grab at something, then scurried back over the barrier and into the bush to hide before their next excursion. There was order, though, to their apparent disorder under the watchful eye of the large male.

She only started her engine when they had climbed the rock face, disappearing into the bush, leaving nothing of themselves behind. She waited, putting off the moment when she would get home and had to tell Owen that she had bought 500 hectares of rough farmland with a darkened, dilapidated homestead and broken-down outbuildings. It was not the Cape Town, the social centre he had in mind for their future. She pulled out of the lay-by and drove off slowly at the thought of what was to come. He would try to draw her into an argument, slam the door on his way out, then she would pass the rest of the evening in silence, waking up to find his side of the bed empty, the sheets untouched.

She wondered if there would be an opportunity to tell him she had known for some weeks that they were going to have a child.

Now, she wants to close her eyes, but she will not. She brings to life the infant that was born to her because these are the things that will keep her in the present. An underwater creature pulled from her. Brown, slippery, swollen eyes, hair slicked to his scalp. The metal and milk smell of him, his tiny baby foot nestling in the palm of her hand, the way his lip arched and thinned as he let out his first cry. The way he looked at her and reached out a hand to her as they lay together for the first time and how she thought that new-born babies were not supposed to have such cognisance. Warm damp baby flesh, she can feel it in her hands now. She keeps the thought, strengthens it. She wants only to sleep and her eyelids fall, but the thought of the boy awakens her. She is with him. She can do this. She must not sleep.

The second time she visited the farm, she was late into her pregnancy. She had agreed to the sale, signed the papers and she was driving out to her own piece of land. Already she had decided this would be her last trip before the baby came. The bumps on the driveway made her put one hand to her stomach as she felt the baby shift. Dust surrounded the car and she shut the window, but the air-conditioning made her throat dry.

The heat was beginning to settle after a wet winter and there was a hot silence over the farm. She walked slowly round the outside of the house, into the tangle of the back garden, and began to make plans as she looked out onto the valley. A dam here to pull water from, vines there. She had been told that roses should be planted to detract aphids from the fruit and she was imagining the fragrance they would create. But as she began to walk down the slope to the reeds, there was another smell which started to make her nauseous. She looked around and saw the wild lilac hanging over the garden wall. Large bunches of flowers dried on the stems, but the leaves were still sage green. The rich, sweet-smelling rot of the dead flowers made her lean against the wall and vomit. And as she left the house, drove her car along the road and out of town, she had to stop again, the smell still lingering as if sticking to her lungs and the lining of her nostrils. She vomited until she retched and there was nothing left inside her, then she wiped her lips, felt a cold sweat on her forehead and sat in the car, her head back against the rest. The first thing she would do when she moved there was dig up the lilac. Even when her hormones returned to normal, she would always associate that smell with rot and decay.

But she forgot the wild lilac. So much had happened by the time she moved to the farm and there was the joy of her new boy, the excitement of transforming and taming the farm and so much to learn and do. Over the years the lilac grew and hung over the wall, scattering flowers, lining the grass below.

When she first moved into the house, she arrived with a bakkie full of possessions: two suitcases of clothes, her coffee machine, a box of food, Finn's high chair, his cot, his feeding equipment, some of his toys, linen and towels from the beach house, a rug she had bought in New York and her computer which she had not opened since leaving America. She hauled a box labelled Photos from the bakkie and she could see the framed pictures resting on the top: her mother and father on their wedding day, a wall-framed photo of her on her graduation day, one of her as a young child sitting with a dog on the lawn outside her family house – she never did call it home – and one of her, sitting in a circle of people she wanted to call friends, Guru in the middle of them. Had her life amounted to those four moments? Was that really the only mark she had made on the world until now? She put the box down and went back for the next one. Owen said he would bring his own things when he was ready. When do you think that will be? she had asked him, but he either did not hear her or pretended not to.

Finn sat in his pram watching as she unloaded onto the stoep, then she wheeled him into the entrance hall as she brought the pieces into the house.

By late morning some men arrived at the end of the driveway; she could see them as she carried and unloaded. They stood in a small group, caps held in their hands, watching silently. At first it made her feel uncomfortable. She noticed each time she returned to the bakkie that they were a little closer and, as they got within view, she could clearly see the man at the front. She thought he looked older than he probably was. His face was grooved and his head was bald, or perhaps it was shaved. He was dark, but not black. He was what they called here Coloured; so were the others.

Need any help, lady? he said, as he came up to the bakkie.

I think I'm fine, she said, but they were still there when she returned for the next box. Thank you anyway, she said.

One of them lit a cigarette and she looked at Finn in his pram.

Needs a lot of work, the older man said, nodding towards the house and perhaps the farm in general.

I've got some plans, she said.

Ahh. They stood silently. The man who was smoking nipped the end of the cigarette off with his fingers and put it in his pocket.

We worked here before, the older man continued.

When Mr Viljoen was here? she asked.

Yes, he said and he shifted his feet. Things have been hard since. Only casual work for me and these boys. We all have families.

She followed his gaze and saw what he saw. A big farm house in need of repair, a garden so overgrown that you could not mow it, a farm so neglected that it seemed it might never yield a crop again and she saw a woman, alone, with a baby in a pram.

There were five of them, all dressed in dark blue overalls. Apart from the one who spoke, the others were young, twenties, she thought.

What's your name?

Raymond, lady.

She held out a hand. Nice to meet you, Raymond. He looked at her hand for a moment then grabbed her fingertips as they shook.

That evening as she prepared Finn's bath, the only sound over the running water was frogs, clicking and croaking. Even in the Catskills she had never known such solitude, there was always the presence of others, the chanting, Guru's voice in the distance.

She closed the taps and took off Finn's outfit, the blue and white sailor top, the linen trousers, and she put them aside. He would not need clothes like that anymore, they were clothes for a city child who did not have the opportunity to play in mud and breathe mountain air.

She remembers now how she dried him, dressed him in pyjamas, remembers his mouth moving on her breast as she fed him in the darkened room she had decided would be his nursery, and she remembers the way his nose moved up and down as he suckled. When she had finished feeding him, she took him into her own bed. His room seemed too far away and too big for someone so small.

The baby in the pram, the naked child in the bath, the soft soapy skin, the starched linen in her hands, his warm mouth on her breast, the warm bundle in her bed, the feel of his breath on her cheek as he slept. She holds these images in her mind, makes them real again. She must piece him together. Every moment, every image, every sensation conjured up is essential, no matter how small.

Over the next few weeks more workers arrived at the farm. By the end of the month there was a group of fifteen. The women followed and the cottages were whitewashed, curtains hung at the windows, a fence was built around the compound and long washing lines were erected. Blue overalls flapped in the wind, dark-eyed children watched from the walls and any time she approached on foot, lean dogs with long, thin tails barked, triggering more barks from other dogs until someone would shout at them to stop.

After the land had been ploughed, technicians came in. They took samples of the soil in Ziploc bags and placed them in the back of a red Toyota. A few days later she received a report which she discussed with Raymond and Piet. The following week the workers' skins turned powdered white as they churned lime into the ground. She filled the shed with bags of wheat, ready to sow between the vines when they were planted, and watched as they ripped deeper into the earth with the hired machinery.

The farm took so much of her time that it was not a conscious decision to keep the house as it was. She used the Viljoens' furniture, the crockery, the cutlery, the glasses and she kept meaning to throw away the old chair by the window, the empty television unit and the few things she knew were too old to live with, but all her energy was concentrated outdoors.

The only thing she did change in the house was Finn's nursery. She dispersed the furniture amongst the other rooms and replaced it with his cot, big green cushions to sit on and a bright blue rug. The walls she painted in the first winter when there was nothing they could do on the farm. By the time she finished, his room was a jungle – a watering-hole surrounded by palms and animals. A giraffe, an elephant, a lion and a zebra all crowded round with smiles on their faces, a monkey hung from a vine above his cot laughing, tail curled.

There was a door leading to his bathroom and she painted the walls deep blue. Fish swam in the ocean amongst coral, a ray, an octopus. Between the mirror and the basin she painted a shark, his large smile showing a row of clean white teeth. She removed the bars from the window over the toilet and she painted a sun around the frame, and on the roman blind a smiley face with puffed-out cheeks.

In May, Finn turned three and they planted the young vines. By the middle of June the planting was finished and saplings poked out of black plastic sheeting in rows all over the valley. The fences were up and wires were taut against wooden stakes, ready to support the stems as they grew. They dug deeper into the dam in front of the house and dug another dam in the north-eastern corner of the farm where mountain water had already begun to fill it. Wheat had been sown between the vines and there was nothing left to do until the first shoots needed pruning. Raymond would be capable of looking after things whilst she was away for a few days. She could find no further excuse for not returning to the beach house.

Owen had been out to the farm on several occasions and he had even left a few clothes in a wardrobe but the last time he came, when he had seen Piet discussing the grape varieties with Raymond, when he had seen the new machinery, the storage shed stacked high with lime and saplings and the sheets of plastic and rolls of wire, he had looked at her and he said, This is a pit. This is a big pit and you – are a fool.

The drive back into town forced her to think about Owen, something she had tried not to do lately. She was leaving the farm because of him and she hated to leave the farm – even if it was only for a couple of days. The farm depended on her in every way – she needed to look at the vines daily to make sure they would grow for her; she needed to look up to the sky and hope for cool mornings, sunny afternoons and light rain in the evenings; she needed to hold her hands together and ask that she be granted the opportunity to make this work and she thought about these things as she drove into town and got nearer to the beach house. Finn snoozed in the back of the car, his elephant pillow wrapped around his neck, his water bottle falling from a sleepy hand onto his lap, crumbs scattered around him from a buttermilk rusk.

She parked her car in the garage at the bottom and climbed the steps to the house. She could smell the distant kelp, the sea air was salty on her lips and the moisture seeped into her hair, weighing it down.

He was sitting at the kitchen table and did not look up at her as she slid the glass doors open.

Have you had breakfast? she asked, as though she had seen him already this morning and was just returning from the bakery. She carried a brown bag filled with croissants and muffins.

He cleared his throat and Finn ran along the hall to see his bedroom.

She put the bag on the table and opened the cupboard, took out a plate. It would be nice if you came back with us, she said, putting the plate on the table, arranging the muffins amongst the croissants.

He raised a glass at her and closed one eye. You've chosen a good business to be in, but a lot of work and not much return.

Wasn't there a time when you thought work was good for you? You were on an 'upward curve' when we met. I think that's the phrase you used.

He laughed. It was loud and she could see the red-wine stains on his tongue. Mad dogs and Englishwomen… he said, slurring his words.

You could come and help at the farm, she said. It's hard work but it's beautiful there.

Help you throw the life we have here into that out-of-town pit? he said, pushing the plate of muffins back into the centre of the table. He picked up the newspaper – it had last week's date on it – and stretched out his legs. Anyway, I have commitments here, he said; then he yawned.

There was only one thing she wanted to take back to the farm with her and she began to look slowly for it as she wandered around the house. She could not call it home – Owen had chosen it from a website in New York and had made an offer on it, site unseen. It's prime real estate, he'd said, and I know real estate. It's a new build in an established area – look at the room sizes, walk-in wardrobes, ocean views, entertainment areas – it's one of the wealthiest suburbs in the world. It's where the elite meet! She mentioned the price. We're lucky to find anything even for sale there, he said to her. He took her hands and smiled.

That smile. She realised later what was behind that smile, but at the time she went along with him because he seemed to know best. He had a strength of character she thought perhaps her father would admire, her mother would approve of. There was nothing wishy-washy about him. He did the deal, knew exactly what she should do at this turning point in her life.

When she reached the lounge, she stopped at the wraparound windows and she stared out to sea. She looked onto the Atlantic Ocean, crests breaking into waves as they rolled onto the beach. A dog ran from the rocks to the water's edge, soggy hair hanging from its belly, its owner in a blue fleece, carrying a lead in her hand, trailing footprints along the shore. It was a view that had lured her many times; the roll of the waves, the glow of the sand, the gentle populace, but the reality was harsh. She had been there, had tried to like it, but the sand whipped into her eyes and scratched her flesh and the water scalded her with its chill.

The large palm at the bottom of the garden had fallen. It was splintered at the base and lay like a drunk on its side. She should call someone to remove it, but what difference would it make?

She walked back into the kitchen, holding a framed photo of herself with Finn on the day he was born.

I'm going to take this back with me, she said.

He looked, not at the photo but at her, his eyes as cold as the grey-green Atlantic. He put down the paper, scraped his chair back on the travertine tiles, picked up the bottle and his wine glass and he walked out of the room.

Under his chair she saw an unopened letter. A handwritten envelope addressed to the beach house with a stamp from America. She would realise later why she had no interest in opening the letter, why she was not curious to read its contents.

The anonymity of New York City had worked for a while. She found an apartment, a job that did not demand too much of her and she was able to melt into something bigger than herself, bigger than her family. I think I need some independence, she said to her mother.

You are a strange child, Victoria, her mother said. Your father won't support you in this venture, you know. He doesn't approve. I know that, Mother, she said. What she did not say was, I know that, Mother, that's why I am going. I need to be away from you all.

It was after a meeting with her boss that she saw the advert in the back of the *New Yorker*. She flicked through the magazine, unable to concentrate on her work. The meeting had unsettled her the way confrontations always did.

How are you finding it here with us, Victoria? he had asked her.

Good. Thank you.

And the work?

I like it.

And do you think you'll apply for promotion after the review? I think you know there's an opening for a senior illustrator.

She looked past his head and out of the window; below was downtown Manhattan but she could only see the roof of the Chinese restaurant opposite. I don't know, she said.

He picked up the file that he was looking at. We usually expect people to push themselves a bit, he said. Shows us we have the right people working with us.

She was not sure what to say. She looked at him and nodded.

Okay then, he said, tapping his pen on the file. Let's set a date for the review, shall we?

The advert featured a black and white photo of a group of people. They were sitting in a circle, holding hands and smiling at the camera. Perhaps she needed to be part of a circle like that. Those people looked so content, so peaceful.

She left Manhattan on a Friday night, along with the rest of the city. Sunset fell over the George Washington Bridge as the cars entered, one at a time, from the Henry Hudson Expressway. Drivers were trying to overtake on the two-lane bridge, the sound of horns, a shout from a wound-down window. The sounds got denser as night fell. Behind her, Manhattan a hazy skyline, the Empire State Building lit up in red, white and blue. In front of her, New York State, clear roads, tall trees, the smell of pines, earth. A soundless evening under a wide indigo sky.

As the rental car wound through the lower Catskills, the darkness, after the city, was complete. With no clear directions, she followed a narrow lane that ran high into the mountain. She passed a lodge with fairy lights at the windows, she passed the ski resort she had been to with work colleagues the previous winter, then the road wound to the left and further up the mountain. At the end of the road, there was a turning. There was no sign, but on the ground there was a whitewashed rock with a single eye painted in the middle.

The front door was wide open and she stood at the entrance with her overnight bag in her hand, wondering whether she should have left it in the car. She took one step forward and entered the room. A fireplace the size of her Manhattan kitchenette, framed by two human-sized pillar candles, burning what? Yes, she recognised the smell. Vanilla essence. Faded armchairs, oversized cushions, rugs covering the floor, all patterns, all colours, fitted tightly together, harmony somehow created out of obvious disharmony.

She followed the soft chanting of voices, through the glass-panelled conservatory and out into the garden, sweeping mountain tops all around. The cool night air brushed over her skin and she left her bag on the step and took her place in the circle.

It was one night in late June that she was woken at four in the morning. Thunder rolled over the house and across the sky so loudly that she sat up, listening for intruders. When her senses calmed and she realised it was a storm, she got up, pushed the window from its frame and let in the night air. The damp earth, newly turned, the woody vapour of young vines, the warm wind of an impending storm. The thunder rolled again, starting from one side of the mountain range and rolling right around to the other. There was a moment's silence before the mountains were lit up from behind with gigantic strobes, sharply illuminating every crevice, ravine and rock. As the light went out, there was a crack so loud it made her jolt and, in that moment, a breeze blew in through the window and pushed the hair from her shoulders.

The cloud canopy was low. Under it, smaller wisps of cloud moved quickly across a stationary moon. A lone ibis flapped rapidly on thick wings, circling high above. What was it doing out at this time of morning, she wondered, and why was it not sheltering from the storm? If she, an alien in this land, knew what was coming, surely an indigenous creature should know.

Within seconds, large drops of rain were starting to fall. One at a time it seemed at first, but soon they gathered speed and began to hit the inside of the glass window. She pulled it back into the frame and went to make coffee.

By seven she had as many buckets, trays, pans and pots as she could find placed around the house. Drops fell into the containers, striking different notes like an orchestra tuning up. She should have known the old thatch would not be watertight and now it would be too late in the season to get a thatcher in. She would go onto the roof as soon as the weather cleared and see if there was anything she could patch up herself.

Finn went from pot to pan, tapping on the sides with spoons, chopsticks, candles, anything he could find. He made up songs and he danced. He took her hand and made her tap one pan whilst he played another. The rain continued. She looked out of the kitchen window to see torrents beginning to run down the mountainsides. Through the wind, she heard the chapel bell. Eleven o'clock, twelve o'clock, one, two, three.

It was late the following afternoon when she put on gumboots and went out into the strange light. She held Finn's hand as they walked down to the dam. Its edges were lost to the water which now lapped against the willows on the higher ground.

She studied the weavers' nests which hung dangerously low over the water. On the short walk down to the dam she had already seen the damage. The black plastic sheeting ripped up, the freshly-turned earth spattered in clumps, and the newly-planted vines ripped from their beds.

Has the storm made problems, Mummy? Finn asked.

Yes darling, she said and she wanted to sit on the wet ground and cry and sob and let the storm out of her own body that had been brewing for so long now.

Has it made you sad, Mummy? he asked.

A bit, darling.

Bad storm. He stamped his foot on the ground. I'm sorry I liked it so much now.

She looked at him. What do you mean?

The storm. I thought it was fun. I like dancing with you. It was cosy at home.

A choking sound came from the back of her throat and she put her hand over her mouth. Then she laughed, suddenly, with tears that fell from the corners of her eyes. She did not have words to explain the feeling behind them and she took hold of her son, his plastic coat squeaking as she picked him up, and she kissed him on his enamel-cold cheeks and he screamed, More! More! So she spun him as well and squeezed him until she had to stop and wipe her nose on the back of her sleeve.

And now, those things are so real to her. Her lips can feel the coldness from his cheeks, her nostrils are filled with the smell of his raincoat, plastic and sharp, her ears hold the sound of his laughter, the noise of a high-pitched boy-child. His hand is wet and warm in hers as they walk through the vines, gathering the stems until the workers arrive with lug-boxes to do the job properly. Her eyes do not blink in case they miss a second of his pale fingers clutching wind-torn saplings as though they were precious jewels and he a miner. These are the details that will bring them together for the journey ahead.

Early one morning in September, she filled her thermos mug with coffee and warm milk and put a sleeping Finn into his backpack and strapped him onto her back. There was a dull end-of-winter sunrise, mist on the dam, over the vines, ghost mountains in the distance. The grass brushed her boots as she walked.

This morning she saw what she had been waiting to see for weeks. The first buds were breaking on the vine stems, already reaching towards the sky. By tomorrow the buds would begin to unfurl into leaves, brand-new and bright green. By the end of the month the wires should be covered in leafy growth. The whole valley floor would be alive with ten thousand stems all growing at once. With that thought she realised there would be grapes. And if there were grapes there would be wine. She had turned this into reality, her reality, Finn's reality. She would have to start being more organised. She had been putting off the accounts, but from today she would have to get a bookkeeper to bring her affairs to order.

She heard the steady rhythm of Finn's breath as his limbs hung loosely around her. She felt the warmth of his body against her back and a pull at the base of her neck. She would not be able to carry him like this for much longer.

As she walked back towards the house, the sun now at the ridge of the mountain, she heard the approach of a deep engine. When she opened the stable door into the kitchen, Owen was there, coffee in hand.

He stood up as she entered and she was not sure what to say.

I've come to help, he said. His eyes were puffy and she was still not sure what to say.

Really?

Yes, he said. Really.

Perhaps she should have said, Welcome, or I'm so glad you've changed your mind, or even, Why have you changed your mind? But everything she could think of sounded artificial and contrived. There seemed to be too much going on for words to be said, so she poured herself coffee, prepared a snack for Finn. There's some fish soup in the fridge if you want that for lunch, she said finally.

When she got back from the vines the following morning there were trucks in the driveway, contractors in the house. The furniture had been moved to the storage shed and by lunchtime a long wall between the kitchen and living area had been knocked out.

If we're going to stay here, we need to make things more comfortable, he said as he handed her a takeaway sandwich. You're crazy to live in an old house like this.

I've been prioritising the vineyard.

You could have hired someone to sort this place out for you.

I've got used to it.

I don't understand you, he said. You act like you're still struggling to pay the rent on a bedsit on 85th and Columbus.

Money can go quickly. The farm has cost a lot. The first harvest won't even begin to pay back what it owes.

It doesn't need to.

It might.

He looked out of the window. How many bottles of wine have you got growing out there?

That's not the point.

He moved closer to her, took her face in his hands. You were left enough money to keep us in luxury for a lifetime. I don't understand – he pointed his hand out to the vineyards, Why all of this? Why all the work? Why can't we just spend and enjoy? He smelled of the takeaway sandwich and she smelled it on her face as he moved away.

We might need to sell the beach house, she said.

He turned and looked at her and she could see it in his eyes, the astonishment. Not yet, she said. But we might have to by the end of the year.

He turned to the foreman who was wheeling a barrow of rubble out of the door. Leave all of this area clear for a fireplace, he said, pointing to the far wall.

By the end of December the house was finished. Owen had asked the estate agent to revalue the house and it now had what she referred to as flow. What a wonderful job they had done, she said. Didn't believe it was possible to bring so much light into this old house. She made notes in her book, clicked her heels on cappuccino sandstone. A wealthy foreign investor could well be interested in this sort of high-end proposition, she said, as she took photos with her mobile phone.

We're not putting it on the market; this is just an exploratory exercise.

Oh yes, she said. I know that. I was just saying...

And now, every time she went into town, people asked her about the house. Her husband had brought so many lovely things it must be quite a showpiece, they said. That was what the local people began to refer to her home as. A showpiece. She was no longer the strange foreign lady who thought she could tame the bush to make wine; she was now the wealthy foreigner who thought she could buy anything and anyone with all her money. Did they call her the Heiress, or did she just imagine that?

She was at the ashram when the news came for her. It was a Sunday afternoon and she was spending her last few hours before returning to New York trying to memorise Guru's book, *Five Steps to Centre Your Mind*. He told her whilst she sat in the glass-panelled conservatory and he placed an arm on her shoulder and kissed her forehead. If you need time to grieve, you may stay as long as you wish, he said. The thought occurred to her that perhaps she should hand all the money over to the ashram, let Guru decide her fate. But then, hadn't she been doing that all her life already, letting others decide what was best for her?

Only she knew what the news really meant and she returned to Manhattan, knowing her life was about to change and that there was nothing she could do about it. With the message had been an instruction to call an appointed lawyer in New York; she should speak to a man called Owen. He would tell her what to do.

Over Christmas, the shiraz grapes turned from green to red. She tried one but spat it out, surprised at its sourness. Shiraz.

She had filled her vineyards with shiraz grapes. Her desire to create the smoky wine had been visceral. She had not drunk any wine throughout her pregnancy and she had thought that, as soon as the baby was born, she would want to savour the drink once more. But as she breastfed, the desire did not return to her. Soon, she thought, when I have finished feeding him, I will know when I am ready. She imagined smoked mussels, fresh bread, roasted tomatoes, blue cheese, the strong food flavours mingling in her mouth with the ruddy wine, but as time passed the desire did not return to her. She had to make a special journey into town to buy a bottle from the store and it stood on the Viljoens' dresser for weeks, amongst the assortment of chipped plates and tea cups, waiting for her. One evening, after she had put Finn to bed, she took the bottle by the neck, sliced the foil with her knife and pulled out the cork. She put it to her nose. Petrol, decayed fruit, wild lilac. She set food out on the kitchen table, poured the wine into a glass. She drank it. The flavour was medicinal, it caught in her throat; wet boots in a hot room, rotting berries, wild lilac.

By late January the fruit was full and hung in large bunches along the bushes. She stood in the central walkway of the valley floor and looked onto the rows of vines. She did not look at individual vines the way she usually did, checking for disease, leaf rot, dryness, size, firmness, maturity, but she looked along the complete rows. They looked like chorus girls, standing in line, arms linked, legs bent under them, tanned stockings, dresses of emerald green with peacock feathers on the shoulders. The more she looked at them the more they seemed to come to life. A light breeze fluttered the skirt hems. The only time she had seen so many dancers together was at *42nd Street* and she could see them now, over thirty girls on the stage together, dancing in unison on the stairs. The sound of the tap shoes, the wind of so many bodies moving together, the feeling that although she was not in the show, for a moment, she belonged to the world where Peggy Sawyer leaves small town Pennsylvania and works her way to the top.

The last time she saw the show she was with Owen. This is your last night in Manhattan, he said. We'll do anything you want. He took her hand and looked into her eyes. This is the eve of our new life together.

She had wanted to share her favourite show with him, she had wanted it to take his breath away the way it had taken hers. He ordered champagne for the interval, the label said Dom Perignon 1985, and although he had not given her the impression that he had enjoyed the show, now, with the theatre bar full of people in diamonds and pearls and real fur and deep-red lipstick, he talked loudly about the performance, holding the bottle, refilling their glasses. People looked at them. His voice was audible above the bar noise, her own silence made it echo more so and she realised she was about to start a new life with this man, was flying to another continent with him tomorrow. He was telling her about a play he had seen recently – before he met her – and she held on to the bar as she thought about how quickly their relationship had progressed, how quickly and easily he had, in his words, given up his life for hers.

Finn was beside her, holding his bucket as they did the late afternoon check. He liked to collect things when they were walking. Feathers, interesting stones, a wild flower that he could press into a book. He was examining a cream-coloured stone that seemed to glitter when he turned it in the sun. He rubbed it between his fingers and turned it some more. Guinea fowl ran through the vines, wings flapping, loose feathers falling to the ground and two geese pulled at the dried wheat stalks. As Finn stood up with his treasure, the geese ran along, flapping until they took off, legs dangling under them. She watched as they separated in the sky. One flew to a single pine, the other into the denser copse. The one on the pine stood silhouetted on a single branch, thick legs under it, crying for its partner. Loud calls, its neck high, until, finally, it threw itself into the air, in search of its missing link with the world.

What are you looking at, Mummy?

Just some birds.

Have you seen this stone?

She looked. It's beautiful.

I'm going to make it into a ring for you.

She crouched down, looked closely at the stone, turned it in her fingers. I think I must be the luckiest mummy in the whole world.

When he smiled, his forehead wrinkled. His cheeks filled out. She could see his milk-white teeth, the slight gap in between the front ones. His skin reddened so slightly that only a mother would notice. He did not put the stone in his bucket, he put it in his pocket and held it there as they walked to Piet's house. Through the shiraz vines, around the new dam at the base of the mountain, through the sauvignon blanc grapes, the voigner that she hoped they could blend for a reasonable young wine.

They drank a bottled beer on Piet's porch and discussed harvest dates. Soon, he said, not yet though. Make sure you have workers ready to pick. We need to pick the moment the grapes turn.

She did not need to look for harvesters. Seasonal workers drifted onto the farm, bringing nothing with them except the hope of a meal and enough pay to see them through to the next job. Men in blue overalls, women in skirts, heads wrapped in cotton, T-shirts with long-since faded logos that sat strangely on bodies they had not been bought for. Nike, Adidas, Aca Joe, Billabong. There was a hostel in town they went to at night, and during the day they came to the farm, waited on walls, under trees; time an elastic thing that seemed to mean little to them.

She looked at the farm's accounts for the first time and it made her feel sick. There were so many things she could not have anticipated; more work than she had expected and more maintenance than she could have predicted. Even if it was a good harvest, even if she managed to get the wine rated and into restaurants and stores, it would be five years until there was a return. When she scrolled to the end of the spreadsheet, there was a minus figure.

She looked up from the computer to the fireplace. Large stone surround, real logs set in the grate, ready to light. The tapestry couches had been handmade to Owen's specifications, the wall lights imported from Bali, the rugs made of Persian silk. A showpiece house. A showpiece house set on a boutique vineyard.

When Piet came to the kitchen door, she was sitting at the table with Finn, crayons, paper, tree bark and coins scattered in front of them.

Come, he said.

She and Finn followed him along the track, past the dam and into the white varieties. He picked one grape from a bunch and handed it to her. He took another and bent over to give it to Finn.

The grape was small, plump but the skin slightly withered. It had the taste of a fresh gooseberry, watery and sweet, and it left a sharp citrusy aftertaste in her mouth.

That's the taste of a sauvignon grape that's ready for harvest, he said. We need to start today.

How long do we have? she asked.

We should start this evening and work through the night. The cooler air will be better to pick in, for the grapes and the workers. Do you want me to tell them?

No thanks, Piet. I'll go.

She bent down as Finn spoke. Can I stay up tonight, Mummy?

He looked at her through khaki-coloured eyes, little flecks of hazel, pupils wide. Please, he said. I promise I'll help.

What would it matter if he stayed up? A night's sleep missed, but a lifetime of experience gained. Wasn't this all for him?

Yes, she said. We'll both stay up – but we have to work hard. All of these grapes need picking. She looked up at the rows of dancers, now covered in precious ornaments. Earrings hanging heavily, necklaces adorning them, bejewelled like divas.

Yippee! He shouted as he jumped up and down on the spot, bare feet disturbing the thick powder of dust under him. You watch, I'll pick faster than anyone!

I'm sure you will, my darling, she said, as they headed towards the workers' cottages, her arm lightly around his shoulder. She felt the lean body under his clothes. He was nearly four but he was strong. There was not the softness of the girls she had known at this age; his flesh was tight over his body, muscles already defined through his stomach and over his back. He was a child, but he was already showing the potential of the man.

As the light began to fade and the frogs' clicking grew louder, she stood on the veranda and watched as the blue tractor was pulled out of the shed, behind it, the wagon loaded high with lug-boxes. Another tractor was already rolling further along the track with the same load. Raymond was at the wheel and a disorganised line of workers followed him, smoke trails above them, hands in pockets, strange languages on the air.

The tractor pulled up. Each man or woman took a box and went along the vines. From disorganisation suddenly came organisation. The ragged line of workers understood the value of timing. As if they had been wound up by a Swiss watchmaker, they began, almost mechanically and with a rhythm that was beautiful to her, to cut, turn, bend and load, each bunch of grapes being laid upon the other, like silk dresses over tissue paper.

Have you finished your spaghetti? she said.

Nearly, he said.

Eat it all up, you'll need your strength, she said.

He nodded whilst he sucked a strand through his lips. There was butter-grease on his chin, some parmesan shavings on the front of his T-shirt.

She can remember so clearly how she took a facecloth from the drawer, ran it under the tap, wrung it out and waited at his side until his pasta was finished. She wiped his face and, when she removed the facecloth, she kissed him loudly on the cheek. He squirmed and giggled the way children do when they pretend they want to escape. He moved his head from side to side, trying to stop her from tickling his neck and she remembers the smell of the butter, sweet and warm, and the parmesan, tangy and ripe.

Her eyes are already closed when she says aloud, I am with you, my boy. And I am nearly ready.

It was fully dark when she took a lug-box from the trailer and she felt the warmth from the engine as they passed it. The floodlights, attached to the tractor, shone over the vines, casting long shadows of the pickers.

She carried the box along the row of workers. They did not turn their heads, but she could sense their attention on her. The strange foreign lady who thought she could tame the bush to make wine or the wealthy foreigner who thought she could buy anything and anyone with all her money? She took some shears from her back pocket and a pair of canvas gloves.

I'll cut, you load. Okay?

Okay, he said. Ready, and he held his arms out in front of him. Her boy was always ready. To walk, to sit, to share, to watch, to wait. There are many things an adult can learn from a child if they are willing to watch and listen, she thought, as she handed him the first precious bunch of grapes and he carried them and bent over the yellow plastic box like a surgeon about to place a heart inside a patient.

The night drew on. The tractors took it in turns to return to the shed so there was always an engine running in the distance. The workers rested in rotas, lying on the cool earth, stretching out their limbs for five minutes until it was time to return to the task. The clouds shifted overhead so that sometimes there was more moonlight than others. The nights were never warm in the Cape and steam rose from the hot bodies that worked silently, cutting and bending, cutting and bending. Raymond worked, then stopped to walk through the pickers occasionally. Cut here, he said to her once, not here, and she adjusted her work.

The talk whittled down to nothing until there was just the coordinated rustle and wind of bodies moving in unison.

She took Finn back to the house at four. He had slept since one in the tractor cab, and was not disturbed as Raymond drove back and forth to the shed.

She could not sleep, knowing the pickers were still at work, but she could not leave Finn alone in the house. She spooned the last of the fresh coffee into the filter and switched the machine on.

She would have to pay the seasonal workers in cash. The wine press would require fifty percent in advance and the invoice for the labels was still outstanding. Over the next month, as the red grapes ripened and the sweeter varieties became ready, there would be more harvesting, more labour, more pressing, more expenditure. Owen was still spending. Clothes, cars, restaurants, wine, but lately, with the time he had spent on the farm, she could only hope that he had begun to feel a connection with what she was trying to do. Perhaps he would understand that they had to put everything into the farm. They could make it work; it would just take time.

The smiley dolphin-face mat is now caked and cold underneath her and she remembers that Owen came home this morning. This morning, was it only this morning? He had a different look about him. What was it? She could not say at first – perhaps it was something of the man she had first met in the lawyer's office in Manhattan, the authority, the purpose. She remembers the mixed feelings she had as he came into the bedroom.

He sat down on the bed next to her, with this new strength of purpose that seemed to surround him, but he did not speak.

The first harvest will be finished tonight, she said.

Still he did not speak.

We worked through the night last night, it was quite something.

Because of his silence, she began to occupy his portion of the conversation. It's too hot to work now. We'll start again later, she said.

His phone rang. It was a new ring tone, she noticed.

He answered it. Yes. That's right. OK. Thank you. You're sure? OK. Good.

He smiled at her. That smile.

The beach house is sold, he said.

The relief brought sudden tears to her eyes. She climbed out of the sheets to get closer to him. She was angry with herself, with her constant doubts and criticism and she turned her body towards him and she touched his arm. She had not even known that he had put the beach house up for sale, but at least he understood and he was showing her that he was prepared to sacrifice his lifestyle until she could get the farm more established.

I've had the money transferred into my personal account, he said. I think you know what that means.

She snatched her arm back, bitten by a snake, then she remembered the letter she had seen under his chair at the beach house that day – the handwritten envelope, the postmark from America.

Amanda contacted me, he continued, as if she had asked for an explanation. She still wants me to go back. Her father has a job lined up for me.

Then she began to remember other things: his near-empty wardrobe, the increasingly frequent overseas trips, his growing anger about the money she spent on the farm, and she remembered the party he had organised at the beach house the week of their arrival. She had been so uncomfortable with those wealthy strangers in her house, and yet after the party she listened as Owen told her what a success it had been and how they were sure to be 'on the circuit from now on'.

So many things she had been almost aware of were suddenly clarified in this one moment. Questions, protests, words, they all balled up in the back of her throat and stuck there and she was unable to move or say a thing as he continued.

I'll fly tonight, he said. I've booked tickets to JFK. I'll leave the car here – a taxi's coming for me. I think it's better that way, less complicated for everyone. And, although he sat there for a further hour, excusing himself, accusing her, it was as if he had already gone. As if he had already picked up his briefcase and walked out of the room.

When he did leave, it was quietly. He left without saying goodbye to her and without saying goodbye to his son.

The night they saw *42nd Street* had been the eve of their new life together. That was what he had said when he took her hands in the bar: This is the eve of our new life together.

He booked them into the Plaza and he lay on one of the king-sized beds in the suite, a *Time* magazine unopened next to him.

Owen, she said, we should go. If we're late we'll miss the first act.

I think this suits us, don't you? he said.

She looked at herself in the bathroom mirror. Yes, she said and she wondered if she smelled of the stale, recycled hotel air.

Owen, she said as they walked through the lobby under the glass chandelier, shall we get a cab or shall we walk?

We'll take the Plaza's car, he said, as he hailed the Mercedes to the entrance.

She realises now why Amanda's letter held no interest for her. Even that night at the Plaza she had known he was just another voice. Someone else to speak for her, instruct her, lead her. But by the time she had realised her thoughts, it was too late.

When the night's harvest was done and the workers had all returned to their cottages and the casual labourers had all walked back into town, she knew that she and Finn would be alone in the house. The Showpiece.

She was inside, door closed behind her when she heard them.

She pushed Finn behind the dresser before they rushed at her. Perhaps they had been waiting all day for her, sure there would be a safe she could give them access to in the Showpiece House. No, she said, I have no jewellery, there is no money. They did not believe her. Look at the house, they said, there must be valuables. No, she said. Take the rugs, take the furniture – that vase, she pointed to the blue Venetian glass that Owen had brought back from his trip to Italy, that's valuable, take it. You think you are funny. You think we are stupid? No, she said. No. She wished there had been a safe; she would have given them everything from it, promised them more, then they might have left. But there was nothing to give them and that made them angry – four angry men and a woman with a hidden child and she knew she was alone – that no one would come to help her.

When they had finished with her, she watched through swollen eyes as they dismantled the house that Owen built. Later, when there was silence – before she was even sure of it – she freed herself, took hold of Finn then dragged her body and his along the passageway and into his bedroom. Jungle animals smiled at them from the darkness of the room, a monkey laughed overhead. She pulled him into the bathroom and the shark teeth smiled down at her from the basin. She locked the door, knowing it would not last under pressure.

Finn cried. Quiet tears rolling down his face as he stood over her.

She lay on the floor, her blood staining the bathroom mat, the happy dolphin face slowly disappearing.

You know how to get to Raymond?

He did not move.

We've walked there so many times. You know the way.

He blinked. Licked his lips. Another tear fell.

She pushed herself up onto the toilet. Stand on here. Put your foot here. But when he did not move she said, Finn! You must get Raymond! and he stood on the toilet seat. Good boy, she said. Now put your foot on my head. He shook his head. Do it! she said. You're too small to reach the window!

She looked up and the last thing she saw was his foot disappearing from sight and she heard the light thump of small bones on dense turf. She wished she had prepared him better for the journey he now faced, alone.

She lies on the floor and she stills her mind. She calms her heart, and she thinks of her son. She begins to conjure him in every way she can.

She must stay with him.

She must guide him in the darkness.

You must look beyond sight itself, close your eyes and centre your thoughts.

British women have backbone, Victoria.

Wishy-washy nonsense.

We usually expect people to push themselves a bit.

I guess that's my way of asking you to light a cigarette for me.

This is the eve of our new life together.

Voices vied for her attention. Shouted at her, demanded that she listen. They had the answer, they all knew best. Listen and learn from me, they seemed to tell her. I am the leader; I will show you how it is. And she went from one to the other, lost as she always had been, until she heard a voice she had heard before but never with this degree of clarity. It was small at first, but as she listened to it the other voices began to fall away.

Have you seen this stone, Mummy? he said.

It's beautiful, she said.

I'm going to make it into a ring for you, he said.

She remembers the stone, unremarkable, cream-coloured but with flecks of gold and pink edging their way to the surface. And she remembers her reply.

I think I must be the luckiest mummy in the whole world.

And she knows.

She is ready.

Can you hear me, child?

I know you can.

I can hear you, see you, smell you, feel you with me.

And I am with you. Never doubt that.

Come now, it is time to start our journey. Hurry because it is a long one and we do not have much time.

Stay with me. We know these paths. We have taken them before.

You remember our walk to the farm cottages that first day? That is the route we will take now. Stand straight, look north, take my hand.

We must cross the grass. Quietly now. You smell that? It is the wild lilac that hangs so heavily. Let it be our shadow as we creep along the wall. Now down to the dam – you see how full it still is? We did well to dig so deep. The weaver chicks have left now, see how the nests hang empty? Now pass the reeds, keep close to them, they will hide us as we move.

Good boy, you have taken off your shoes. Now crawl over the bridge my darling, do not risk being seen. Hear how the river runs? The noise will cover us as we move.

We will take this track to the left, be careful of the sharp stones, tread lightly. The track splits twice before we reach the cottages, we must stay left. But you know that, my clever angel.

We are walking so fast, our feet are almost running under us. We will be there in no time.

See how we glide? It is like we are flying over the grass, now higher, the vines skimming the soles of our feet.

Can you smell the gooseberry of the grape leaves? The air is fresh with it. But these shiraz grapes will be the best. See how many the workers are gathering? Our wine will be remembered forever. The fruits are so dark, the skins so velvety, the bunches so full that they strain on the vine.

Your hand feels warm in mine, do not let go, we are nearly there. Our house looks so small. Our house, our home, our castle, our place on earth. I have built it for you. I built an oasis in the desert. And you, so young but so nearly a man. To see you, I am proud. You know these paths; we have walked them before. Do not stop now; we are nearly there.

Can you hear me, child?

I know you can.

I can hear you, see you, smell you, feel you with me.

And I am with you. Never doubt that.

Do not stop, my child. You are nearly there.

FREEDOM; ONE DAY AT A TIME

Lock door. Quiet. Dark. Alone. Sticky fingers. Crisps. Headache. Damp. Flat. Smell. Body.

Not tired, but tired. Tired of trying so hard, so much, so long.

They all came tonight: Lara, Jasmine, Eric. All that crowd. Looking up, thumbs up. Smile back. Others. Faces, yes. Names, no. Fifteen years. Couldn't talk to them tonight. Don't know what to say anymore.

Any interest yet? Agent? Deal? Album, YouTube?

I laugh, *One day at a time.* That's the song they love.

Why isn't it a hit yet?

What can I say?

I haven't got it in front of the right people? I'm too old? I'm too old and too tired. Tired of trying so hard, so much, so long.

Or maybe I'm just not good enough.

Tessa kisses Rob before he sits at the drum kit. She kisses him and looks at me. She smiles and waves. Yeah. I know what she's thinking. I tune up, plug in my pedal.

Fifteen years of support. Friday nights, Saturday nights, mid-week nights, empty warehouses, sold-out festivals, warm-up gigs, local media.

I've let them all down. They've given me so much and I've given them nothing in return.

I want them to have their 'I-told-you-so'. Tell their friends – we were right to back her all the way. We knew!

But still. No interest, no agent, no deal, no album, no YouTube.

What's their payoff for tickets, petrol, time wasted? They'll stop coming. They'll give up on me. Or maybe I'll give up first.

Take it, take it, take it – One day at a time.

My voice. I can hardly hear it anymore. But I can feel it. It melts into and over the guitar chords and I can feel it resonate in my chest and rise into my throat. My fingers on the fret, the wood around my body. The steel on my fingertips. Nails blunt, fingerprint erased. It's all I have left. This. Here. Now.

Headache. Damp flat. Smell.

Wine in fridge. Good. Cheap. Fine. Drink quickly. Relief. Fill again. Sit. TV to numb my brain.

Tessa. The drummer's girlfriend. Younger. Better. Fresher. She can do it. She knows it. She wants it. They want her. But it's been so long. The band don't know how to ask me to move over.

I should let go first. For all of us. Ten years and nothing. Keep on or give up?

Desk job. End of life. I can't do that and I can't do this. But if not this, then what? This is all I know.

I love them. The band, the crowd. Nothing else will bring that. I am them and I am me and I am this and I am here and this is it.

Another bottle at the back of the fridge. Screw top. Bring to couch, save getting up. Hate this TV show. False characters. Canned laughter, exhausting. But if I concentrate on this, I might forget me.

I've been 35 for too long now.

This TV woman. Botox. Can't smile. How can she act with no expression?

HaHaHaHa. HaHaHaHa. Canned laughter. Laughing at me sitting here. Alone. Quiet. Dark. No Botox. Getting older.

Better, younger ones waiting to replace me. Band afraid to ask me to move on. No agent, no deal, no album, no YouTube. Nothing to show. Only just making rent. The crowd will leave. Because I'm going nowhere and I can't make it work. I can't!

I switch. Fucking talent shows. They're everywhere. Vodka somewhere. Bring to couch, save getting up.

Sixteen-year-old stars. Sing-a-song, TV-friendly. No Botox required. Win, not win, contract, agent, album, YouTube, money.

My crowd should start watching TV. Vote for winners. Better odds. I don't even want the fame. I just want this. To. Work.

No more mixer. Fine. Ice. Can't be bothered to get up. Warm vodka. Driving round the country with PA, guitar, microphone. Cash in, cash out. Crisps for dinner. Live alone. Always alone.

Headache. Eyes sore. It won't happen now. Spill on couch. Whatever. Tablet will help. Two better. Smile like woman on TV. Nutter with Botox. Perfect house. Red dress. Drink them down. Two more. Keep going because if some is good then more is better.

We followed her everywhere and she never made it. Waste of space.

Band wants me to go.

She wants my place. I'm too old. Can't wait forever.

Letting them all down.

There's always a winner on a talent show. But in real life nobody wins, nobody loses; we're all just here, filling in the gaps, passing the time. There's nothing coming. No one's coming. Highs are high. Lows are low. So quiet. Just me. Pills. Bottle. Tired. Me and the perfectly preserved woman who will stay trapped on that programme forever. She'll be there and I'll be here, on the couch. Forever. Canned laughter. Just for me.

She never made it. She just didn't have it.

All or nothing.

All.

And.

Nothing.

Quiet. Dark. Alone. Not tired, but tired.

Tired of trying so hard, so much, so long.

★★★

'Callie? It's Adele.'

'Adele? What the –? You know it's 3 ay em here? Jeez. I thought my mother was dead.'

'Sorry. It can't wait. Al Klubcar was there and I know he's making the same call to his people right now. I need you to wake up and I need to tell you something.'

'OK. Wait a minute. I've had a few. Let me get up and get straight. I'll call you in ten.'

'Make it nine,' I say.

She puts the phone down and my heart's still beating hard. My hands fidget whilst I wait.

Never had this before. Something close but not this. I grab a beer, no. Too late, too early, I need a clear head. Herbal tea.

Okay, make notes before Callie calls back.

Those talent shows are over. It's been coming and I've been waiting. A long time. Only the producer wants those acts. That safety. It doesn't reflect emotions anymore. It's cyclical, the world's changing. The music is about the people. The now. The struggle. The times. I remember it from the 60s. What happened to all of that? Where did it go? Music holds up the mirror and lets people see themselves reflected in the artist.

And she's it. She's the mirror. Raw energy right on the line. You don't even know if she's going to finish the fucking set, it's so real! The whole thing. The music, the progressions, the lyrics. But her face when it comes together. She's everyone and no one. And I've just found her in some crappy bar in Cape Town.

Come on, Callie, that's seven minutes and I'll bet Al Klubcar is on the phone to his people right now, squeezing a number out of them. But this one's mine. She's it and I've found her.

I dial again.

'Didn't I tell you I'd call you back?'

'I can't wait. She's the one Callie. I've found her and we've got to do this now or Al Klubcar will be over there tomorrow with his stylists and his deal and we'll miss it. Callie – I've been doing this for fifty years and I tell you, I don't even mind missing my commission on this one, but you have to give me something to take to her first thing.'

'Oy, Adele. Slow down. Okay. Send a file over. I'll listen.'

'I don't have one and I haven't got time to mess around! Give me an offer now. This is it. She's the mirror. They'll all see themselves and she'll shine the light and they're going to love her.'

Callie's quiet and I can hear my own panting breath. I'm too old for this game but I don't care, I can still feel it and I'm not giving up yet.

Finally, she says, 'I'm gonna send you a number and you can take it to her now or in the morning or whatever the hell else you want to do with it. Mirror. Jeez, Adele. You're getting senile, you know that?'

'Yes, I know it. But I'm not stopping. Make it a good number. A better one than Al Klubcar will take her.'

'Let me sleep, crazy old woman.'

I'm still panting when I read Callie's message.

OK, that's a number I can take to her. I'll wait a couple of hours. Musicians hate mornings but I think she's going to like tomorrow morning. The message with that number and a two-record deal. That's a good morning even if it's early.

I sit and wait and I don't sleep and at seven I start calling. And I wait for her to pick up. I call again. Musicians, all the same.

By ten o'clock she must have twenty missed calls from me. I call the Cape Town bar and ask for her address, but they don't have it and then I end up calling everyone I know, but I can't get any info on her. I stay on my phone, calling, scrolling, searching.

Then later, I see the Facebook post from that bar.

RIP Jo Stanley who took it One Day At A Time.

Thanks for choosing The Feathers for your final song…

I sit on the couch and I cry. I cry for myself and I cry for her. I cry because I've been around long enough to know that people like Jo Stanley, they don't come around twice in one lifetime.

Jo Stanley.

She hadn't even started and she's already gone.

TRADE

A girl stands in a doorway. She is waiting for something to happen, hoping that it will not. She has nowhere to go. Her head moves as she watches people pass her. Busy people, smart people. The sort of people she has never seen before. It is nearly Christmas.

A man walks by, then he takes a step back. Are you okay? he asks her. She does not reply. I asked if you are okay, he repeats and she tries to hold herself up. If you want to be like that then fine, he says, and he takes a note out of his pocket, folds it and gives it to her. She knows how to take money and she presses it into her bra before he changes his mind.

Luca sat on one of the brown chairs and waited, her hands folded in her lap, her knees together, feet parallel. She would have liked to wait here all night, letting the other girls leave and come back while she waited. But, as she had learnt, waiting brought trouble, and Luca did not want trouble. Working hard, keeping eyes down, being quiet, obeying rules. These things did not bring trouble. If you were lucky.

A film of sweat gathered between her thighs and the plastic chair and as she moved one leg to cross it over the other, the sole of her shoe stuck for a moment on the carpet.

Luca.

She heard the sound of her name. The woman's voice high, sharp, the sort of voice that reached into you and warned you that it would be back, soon.

She stood up. Walked through the waiting room and into the hallway, narrow, dim. The sound of the man's footsteps fell behind her as they walked, single-file. She did not turn around, but she listened. Quick steps, feet that barely touched the ground, clothes that made no sound, breath that was snatched from the air. She had learnt that you can tell many things about a person before you look at them. Maybe I am becoming Streetwise, she thought. That was the word Tanya had used, Streetwise. You think you are so Streetwise, Luca.

She opened the door. That smell. She wondered if she smelled of it. Rancid cheese, a facecloth that had been left on the sink for too long, unwashed hair.

People brought their bodies to this place because there were pieces of themselves they could no longer carry. They came here with their loads weighing on them, shoulders tight, neck strained, backs bent. They took Luca and gave her their load so that when they left they were light again, free of the little pieces they could no longer carry. But for them to be this way, Luca had to carry the load. Load upon load, weight on top of weight, until she felt as though she walked with stones in her shoes, concrete clinging to the strands of her hair, lead lining her clothes. For them to walk freely she had to be this heavy.

Natalie had once asked her, If you had one wish what would it be?

Only one? she had asked.

Just one.

To marry a prince.

Even when she said it she knew it was a waste of a wish and as soon as it was spoken she wanted to say, No, wait. I've changed my mind. I want to finish school, go to university, learn things so that I can be clever, go overseas, get a job, send money home, make my mother smile. But Natalie had told her just one wish, so she had let it be.

When Romolo came she remembered that wish and she tried to think back to the day she had made it. Was it a full moon? Had a star fallen out of the sky? Had she been standing at the end of a rainbow? Could it really be a wish come true?

The first time she saw him she was walking back from the factory. They had told her there would be work. She kept asking when. Soon. How soon? Try again next week.

If she walked quickly it took her forty minutes to get home, but today she walked slowly, with no news, and as the grit from the path entered her boots, it rubbed her toes. Months ago some government workers had driven up in yellow trucks and left piles of concrete slabs, piles of metal rods and bags of cement along the road. There was going to be a proper road, with a path at the side of it for people to walk on. Too many deaths on such a dangerous road, it had said in the newspaper. But weeks passed and no one came to build. The bags of concrete disappeared, the stone slabs went missing in the middle of the night, and what remained of the iron rods were rusted and bent from the children's games.

Luca stopped to empty her boot. With her toe pointing to the ground and her arm out to balance herself, she held the boot upside-down and shook it from the heel. She looked up as tyres crunched slowly on brown dirt. She stopped shaking, held the boot closer to her body and saw the shiny car, bright and red against the brown and grey of Zirsk. The man inside turned his head and smiled at her from behind tinted glass and she stood, toe pointing to the ground, arm out to balance herself, boot held upside-down and her foot came down into the dirt and the grit. As the car drove off, she lifted it quickly and put her boot back on and she thought to herself, If I had known I was going to see a handsome prince in a horse-drawn carriage,

I would have put on my ball dress. The thought made her smile, but then it turned quickly to sadness when she realised that she could not share this story with Natalie.

She made her usual stops on the way home. The store, no situations vacant; the laundry, nothing today; the bar, we are a family business; the butcher, this is man's work; then she took the long walk up the hill, past the houses, which got smaller and shabbier as she wound her way to the top. Every night, the factory smoke rose and settled over the highest houses before seeping into the empty valley to the other side.

By the time she got home, the house was under a night sky. She pushed the front door open and smelled the remains of wood smoke from the grate. Her father snored lightly on the sofa and both the bedroom doors were closed. She poured a mug of water and sat at the kitchen table. The water was cold in her warm mouth and it tasted hard and metallic.

If there was another factory, she could ask them for work, but there was only one factory in Zirsk and just eighty people needed. The week before, Luca heard a woman had sliced her finger off in the canning machine. She waited in line with more women than she could count – and some men too, even though everyone knew the canning factory was women's work – but the woman was already back at work, having promised production would not drop with nine fingers. Luca went to bed that night and prayed the woman's production dropped and her job would become available. Then, as Luca rolled onto her side and pulled the blanket over her head to block out the sound of her little brother's snores, she wondered when other people's bad news had started to become her good news.

When she awoke later in the sooty darkness, she sat up silently in bed, put her hands together and closed her eyes. Please forgive me, dear God. Please look after the woman, Eva, and her family and make sure they have food and that she keeps her job and that her finger is not too sore when she works. And, dear God, I am sorry to ask again, please help me to find work. If you help me to get a job, I will work so hard and give up my own freedom so that I can bring money into our house.

She opened her eyes for a moment and watched her sister sleep. She stroked her hair, slightly damp at the forehead, away from her face. She had another request and she thought about how to ask for the right thing in a way He would understand and approve of. But she was not sure that God would want to give her a job, a husband and happiness all in one prayer, so she finished with an amen and lay back down to listen to the night noises that thickened the air around her. The wind that rattled the door in its frame, the tree that scratched at the kitchen window, perhaps asking to come in from the cold, the soft breaths of her sister as she slept beside her. If Luca could bring some money home then her sister could finish school. Not many girls got to finish school in Zirsk; too many chores to be done at home, another pair of hands always needed, not enough money for books. She lay close to the child and felt her warmth. I hope she is dreaming of good things, she thought.

Still no job, Luca? her mother asked while they made breakfast together.

No, Mama. Still no job. They say maybe next week.

Her mother stirred a pot. Added water, stirred some more. The porridge was heavy and her cheeks were bright. With her headscarf tied over her head and knotted in the old-fashioned way at the base of her neck, and her apron tightly tied over her stout body, she could have been a woman twice her age. I remember a time when she was beautiful, Luca thought, and she was aware that she had inherited her mother's strong nose, wide-set green eyes and high cheekbones. But her mother's eyes had deepened in their sockets, her cheeks had become veined, her skin was now sallow and Luca thought, This is what a life in Zirsk will do to a beautiful woman.

Her mother took a pinch of salt from a heavy ceramic bowl and rubbed it with her thumb and forefinger over the pot. She looked into it as she stirred.

Natalie's mother was in the store yesterday, she said.

Luca listened and watched.

A basketful of food, she said, beginning to nod her head as her shoulder worked a large circle around the pot. Beads of sweat began to show on the older woman's forehead. Foreign ham, cheese, two loaves of bread, some beer. She made a noise from the back of her throat. Pushed to the front of the queue and put it on tick. So now, if you have money, life is free. You see? This is what happens when your daughter finds work in another country.

Luca opened the kitchen window. The chill reached into the room and cut through the heat of the stove.

She had not seen Natalie for two weeks now, but for at least four weeks before that they had seen very little of each other. It was as if Natalie had found a new life and had cut Luca out of it completely.

Clouds hung in the sky. Dense and bluegrey they promised snow and she thought it was going to be a long winter.

What are you looking at?

Nothing, Mama.

Then shut the window, Luca. Shut it.

He put his lips on hers. She tried to turn her head; she did not like to kiss. His lips were thin and dry and she felt them chafe her cheek. He pecked at her like a hen pecking for grain on a dusty floor. Then he turned her around.

There was a story. She closed her eyes tightly and tried to remember. It was the one her mother used to tell her at bedtime when she was small. Before her brother and sister were born, before her mother had become too tired for bedtime stories and too old before her time.

It was a special voice she used, an end-of-day voice. Quieter, closer. She lay down next to Luca and left her shoes on the floor, side-by-side on the mat. She looked up at the ceiling as she spoke and Luca remembered the story so well, remembered the way she had felt when her mother spoke to her as they lay in bed together, like the shoes, side-by-side. She closed her eyes tightly.

Many years ago, her mother always began, there were two rulers, the King and the Green Emperor. They lived at each end of the earth and in between them was wasteland where nothing would grow and no man could live. The King had three sons, but the Green Emperor had none, so the Emperor wrote to the King, promising his kingdom to the son that would join him. The oldest and the middle brother failed to even cross the bridge out of their own kingdom and the King was so angry at their failure that the youngest prince ran, frightened and crying, into the palace garden.

Why was he crying, Mama? Luca asked once.

Because, said her mother as she turned her head to Luca, he knew he must prove himself to his father, like every child must prove the cost of raising them has been worthwhile.

Luca waited in silence, wanting to know the rest of the story, but afraid for her mother to go on. Her mother looked back up to the ceiling. A beggar woman came into the garden, looked at his hand, told him his fortune. She told him he would inherit great riches and become a glorious emperor, but first he had to ask for his father's old stallion, ragged clothes and rusty sword. With those old things, he rode into the wasteland.

Why did he go? Luca always wanted to know. He was a prince, he had everything he wanted, why would he risk so much? But when she found out that the stallion could fly and talk and that his clothes were sewn with armoured thread and the weapons were sharp, she felt better for him.

As he passed over the bridge, her mother said, the King gave him a blessing – but then he warned his son: Beware of evil! You must beware of the Bald Man!'

Luca hated it if her mother stopped there for the night. If she turned off the light and left Luca alone in bed, she could never think about the happy ending she knew was to come, she could only think of the Bald Man.

★★★

Luca opened her eyes. He did not look at her as he stood up. They never did. The urgency had left him and he wanted to leave the room quickly, to be away from her, from what he had done. He threw a tissue on the mattress next to her and closed the door behind him.

She cleaned up and walked back along the hallway. If I was a man and I wanted to pay for these things, she thought, I would not pay for a filthy place like this, with dirty mattress, floorboards, paint coming off the walls, bad smell. What person pays to be here? But there was never an answer to her question, just faces, bodies, odours, noises, the waiting room, the hallway, the workroom.

The only chair in the waiting room was next to Tanya. Luca had no choice and she sat on it and listened as the girl's breathing quickened. Her own heart began to move faster in her body and Madame stood up from behind her desk and looked at Tanya then at Luca. Her look was enough. Luca lowered her eyes to her knees.

★★★

As Luca walked back up the hill with her mother, the older woman's breath became shorter and, as she spoke, steam escaped from her mouth. Luca could not help looking up each time a car passed. For Natalie's mother, credit, but for us, top price wanted! her mother said. She shook the bag of flour in her hand, roughred from the cold and the housework.

Luca pushed the front door of the house open and the smell of her father's stale body caught her. He lay on the sofa, his bad leg resting on a cushion. He had been on the sofa for weeks. He slept there, ate there, waited there as though a miracle might come in through the kitchen window and save them all.

Her mother removed her coat, folded it over the arm of the sofa and adjusted her headscarf. She put the flour on the table then turned to the cupboard, took out a large bowl and a glass jug and put them down next to the flour. And then, as if forgetting what she was doing, she sat down on the kitchen stool, her legs slightly apart, and put her elbow on the table, her forehead resting in the heel of her hand. When she spoke, Luca was not sure who she was speaking to.

How can I feed you all? Your father will not work again. No work to be found for Luca, no work to be found for an old woman like me. What am I going to do? A man and three children to feed.

She looked up and her eyes met Luca's and Luca looked away.

They left the dough to rise in the darkened cupboard whilst they got ready for evening church. There would be fresh bread with soup for dinner and Luca felt their mood lift as they left the house. This was the time of day when they could do something to help themselves. There was a God and they could pray to him.

After the service they stood at the church gates. They greeted their neighbours and shared their news. Gloved hands held each other for moments whilst they spoke of the weather – Yes, it will be a cold winter – and spoke of work – They said they may take more workers next month, Yes they say that every month but we still wait and hope – and they spoke of missing friends – How wonderful that Natalie has found work overseas! I always said she was a special girl, very clever! And her mother, what fortune!

The Rector came to the gates to talk with his congregation as he did after every service. As he moved into the gathering, he stepped towards Luca and touched her arm, a light touch, soft fingers.

Natalie's family feel blessed that she has found work overseas, he said.

Yes, she has been lucky.

You must miss your friend.

Luca shrugged and looked at her mother talking to Madam Domenza.

Still, he continued, there are merits in a home life, to knowing one's neighbours and friends. Luca nodded, thinking of Natalie, already working in another country, perhaps a new boyfriend, foreign clothes. And to recognising one's enemies, he said. Luca smiled at him, feeling too tired all of a sudden for conversation. Sensing perhaps that she would not listen for much longer, he said what he had come to say: Remember, Luca, to believe in God is to believe in the devil and we must always watch out for the devil, who can take many forms.

Thank you, Father, you gave a beautiful service tonight, she said. Thank you.

★★★

Tanya's leg was so close that she could feel the heat coming from her skin. Her own body felt hotter as she sat next to the girl. You think you are so Streetwise, Luca. You will see. That was what she had said on the first night. You will see.

Luca did not know how long Tanya had been there, but she knew she had been there long enough to know the rules and how to use them. Don't expect to make friends here, Luca. In another place she might have been giving her advice. An old girl at school, helping a new girl. But the voice she used, the way she whispered in the dark, words hissed through closed teeth – it was not the way one girl would make another welcome.

Tanya got up and walked to the doorway. It was a busy night. Every night was a busy night. When she first came, Luca had kept note of which day of the week it was but, as the days went by, there did not seem any point in knowing if it was Tuesday or Sunday. There was no weekend to mark the end of the week and nearly every day was the same. She did not like to think about the days that were not the same. She never knew when they were coming and she lived with the fear of not knowing when to anticipate these days.

She saw a finger point at her and again she had to leave the safety of the brown seat. Along the hallway. Heavy footsteps behind her. Thick breaths through an open mouth, denim trousers brushing together, the sound of a belt buckle as she opened the door, a large hand on her shoulder pushing her against the wall.

Her English teacher at school had been called Mrs Smith. That was not her real name, but that was what the children had to call her during class time.

Good morning, Mrs Smith.

Good morning, children. What is your name?

My name is Luca.

Do you have the time, please?

Yes. It is half past three.

How old are you?

I am eight years old.

Can you tell me the way to Piccadilly Circus?

She remembers thinking how exciting Piccadilly Circus sounded. Mrs Smith showed them pictures of a tiny statue on top of a large plinth holding an arrow. Eros, she said. The God of Love. Natalie and Luca exchanged looks. People passed by the statue holding umbrellas, wearing raincoats. Younger people sat on the steps at the bottom of the statue. There were pigeons, cars, shops, neon lights. It was a world Luca could only imagine from that photo. They learnt about other things too. The greatest band in the world, The Beatles, the richest woman in the world, the Queen, the most important writer in the world, Shakespeare. The Sixties, miniskirts, Punk Rockers, Abba, Duran Duran, a cup of tea in a real china cup, cucumber sandwiches, roast beef and Yorkshire pudding, cheddar cheese.

The man with the thick breath pulled himself away from her. Pulled up his jeans and left without asking the way to Piccadilly Circus. She had been in England, maybe even London, for many days and nights and no one had asked her name. Where was this Britain she had learnt about?

★★★

Natalie was still not in the waiting room. She had been lying down earlier, rolled on her side. Luca had thought she was asleep, but when she looked again, she saw that her eyes were open and that she was staring at the wall, arms wrapped around herself.

'Natalie,' she had whispered. 'Natalie.' But she had not responded. Luca had wanted to lie down with her, to be close to her, but Tanya was there, watching from the corner like a vampire in an old black-and-white film.

Leave the little bitch, she said. She will get us all into trouble with this diva behaviour.

Luca wanted to stroke her hair. Remind her of something real. But she heard Madame coming along the hallway.

Why are girls not in waiting room? she shouted. Move. Now.

★★★

Romolo.

Everything she had dared to dream about.

The prince in shining armour that every girl secretly hoped would rescue her from the tower. Her own fairy-tale prince.

New clothes, a pair of gold earrings, a box of food for her mother, a bottle of whiskey for her father, chocolate coins for her brother and a music box for her sister. Trinkets that smelled of another place. A place that was clean, new, that had not yet been covered by the grime of Zirsk that eventually tainted everything that came to it.

She was on the way to the factory to look for work again when he stopped her.

Do you want to come in my car?

Luca looked around to see who he could be talking to.

You, Little Sparrow. Would you like to come in my car?

It was so clean, and she had never seen anyone in a red car before. The cars in Zirsk were beige, brown, dark green. This car could be seen against the backdrop of the grey buildings like a robin's breast against snow.

Yes. Please. Luca looked at her dusty boots as she folded her legs into the passenger seat. She could smell leather from the car and something else from him. Warm spices, a deep smoky scent with something like lemons that cut through.

Where are you going? he said.

To the factory. I need to find work.

Work is very hard to find.

Yes. It is. It is very hard to find.

Today, you should not look for work. A beautiful girl like you needs a holiday. I will take you.

Yes, thought Luca. A holiday sounds nice. Even though she had never had a holiday and was not even sure what one was.

Romolo drove her forty minutes out of Zirsk. He did not talk on the way; he drove fast and he played the radio loudly. Loud songs in a dead town.

But as they left Zirsk and the road became wider and the sky above her seemed to clear, she began to enjoy the music. She recognised one of the songs, 'In the Name of Love', and she sang the chorus quietly to herself under the noise of the engine.

She did not understand the lyrics but she knew what the word 'love' meant.

They sat by the canal for two hours. Romolo had brought a bottle of brandy and some diced meat and cheese. The wind cut through her coat and the flesh on her legs was so cold that she could feel the hairs poke through her tights. But she did not dare to complain about the weather, she did not want anything to break the spell that surrounded her this afternoon. She did not want to make a man like Romolo think she was complaining and ungrateful. She drank the brandy from the bottle and chewed on the meat until he opened the car door for her and drove back along the dark roads to Zirsk. His cell phone rang, a noise like a fly buzzing on the dashboard, but he let it ring. Who wants to do business when there is a beautiful woman in the car? he said. She smiled and settled back into the deep leather of the passenger seat.

The drink made her feel more comfortable in his presence and she was happy to laugh at his jokes on the way home, about men he knew, things they had done, tricks they had played on each other. It felt like a long time since she had laughed and she laughed perhaps more than she would have done if it was someone else telling the story. Someone whose hair was not so black, whose eyes were not so brown, whose skin was not so tanned. She watched his hands on the wheel. Large hands, strong but clean with square nails and soft hair between the knuckle and the finger joint.

★★★

As she sat in the waiting room, she wondered if anyone could tell if she prayed. If she did not close her eyes and she did not kneel and she did not bring her hands together, would they know she was praying? And if she did pray like this, she wondered, would it really be a prayer and would He hear her?

★★★

Get up, Luca, her mother called to her. Get up. There is a man waiting for you at the door. Her mother had an almost-smile on her face which Luca had not seen for a long time. She did not usually sleep in late, but after the brandy yesterday her head felt uncomfortable and she had spent a night trying not to wake her siblings next to her. Instead of their closeness bringing comfort, last night they had brought only heat; a heat from which she could not escape whichever way she turned.

She was embarrassed when she saw Romolo at the front door. She felt the way she might feel if she walked into a smart clothes shop in the city with her overalls on. Her hair was knotted, her skin pale with circles under her eyes and her pyjamas were a pair of faded tracksuit bottoms and an old school T-shirt.

Her mother was listening from the kitchen area. Luca knew she was pretending to work so that she could find out what the arrival of this man meant.

I bring a gift, said Romolo.

A gift?

Yes. A gift. To say thank you for spending the afternoon with me yesterday. I was cheeky to ask you and I hope you forgive me?

Of course, said Luca, but she thought, Why is he sorry? Is he ashamed we went out together?

For you, he said as he pulled out a small packet with pink paper and a soft ribbon. She opened it and looked inside. It was a blouse. Not the sort of blouse she could get at the local store; the grey and white blouses or the dark blue work shirts that she borrowed from her father. She ran her hand over it. This was fine material that felt like butterfly wings on the skin. There was a frill around the neck, a little puff at the top of each shoulder. The fabric was white and green and there was a delicate flower embroidery pattern that ran in straight lines from top to bottom.

Green to match your beautiful eyes and white to match your perfect skin, he said.

Her mother made a noise from the back of her throat and Luca turned to see her throw a ball of dough onto the kitchen table and begin to scatter flour over it.

And, he said, if you will permit, something for your mother? He pushed another packet towards Luca and she took it and walked the few steps to the kitchen table to hand it over. Her mother wiped her hands on her apron and took the packet, shinyblue in her roughred hands. She held it in front of her as if it contained dynamite and to open it might be to light a match.

Please, madam, open it, said Romolo.

My mother is blushing, thought Luca. I do not think I have ever seen her do this. She felt proud to be the one to bring this man into the house that made her mother's cheeks red.

I should not accept. I do not know you… her mother said.

Please, do not insult me, Romolo said, a smile on his face.

The older woman crinkled the packet, tore off a corner and looked inside.

Luca could see her sister and brother at the bedroom door.

Her mother held her gift up to examine it. A scarf. Not like the scarves she usually wore on her head; rough woven fabric, darned, faded, tied tightly at the base of her neck. This was a silky material in skyblue and lemonyellow. Surely there had never been such things in Zirsk before?

I do not know what to say, said Luca's mother. Her eyes were moist and she rubbed her nose with her thumb. Loose specks of flour fell from her hands onto the new fabric and, as she went to brush it away, a thread caught on her roughred thumb and pulled the scarf tightly together from corner to corner.

Oh! No! I am so sorry. I am so clumsy. Such a fool! The scarf fell as she released it, the skyblue and lemonyellow lying on the rough cement of the kitchen floor.

★★★

Luca recognised the man in the green coat. She lowered her eyes, trying not to show her face. But she knew without looking that he had seen her and she heard her name called by Madame.

Luca.

And then she was walking the hallway on legs that felt like they were balancing on stilts and with a head that felt like it could float away from her body. Slow footsteps behind her. A click of the heel. Long heavy breaths, a coat being removed, a thick dense fabric, the sound of fingertips rubbing over chin stubble.

She had to make a certain amount of money every night – all the girls did – it was in the rules. Luca had learnt from Madame on her first night that there were many rules here.

Girls must work hard.

Girls must always look sexy.

Girls must keep customer happy.

Girls will not have day off.

Girls will work whenever they are told to.

Girls will wash every day.

Girls will clean up after customer.

Girls will not talk to customer or complain.

Girls will not accept gift or ask to borrow cell phone from customer.

Girls will not take money from customer.

Girls will cover up bruises, bites, scratches.

Girls will not talk to each other.

Girls are very lucky to have such good work opportunity.

Girls will line up here to see how much they owe for journey to England.

Luca had been told that she would be charged for transport, accommodation, chaperone, visas, passports, uniform, make-up, food, drink – the list was so long and she was not very good at reading, but she had understood that the amount she owed was more than her whole family could earn in the factory for a whole year, two years, perhaps three, but she could not work it out in her head.

Madame Povrovski had pointed to an open book in front of her as she stood in the doorway of the girls' sleeproom. Deductions will be made every week for expenses: food, clothes, accommodation, protection, et cetera, and what is left will go to pay off debts. The book was black, with a hardcover and red writing on the front. She had snapped the book shut and held it against her chest. What was inside was only for Madame to see. Luca was told, not shown, what she owed. There had been no slip of paper given to her explaining the amount she owed, no calculator displaying a number that she could see.

Madame had turned to walk away, then she spun back to look at each of them in turn. She spoke quickly and suddenly. Any girl who tries to escape will be brought back and debt will be doubled.

Luca thought she might fall over and she put her hand on the wall to steady herself. She wanted to ask how much money she would earn in a day so she could work out how long it would take to pay off the debt. When she thought of that now, she realised how stupid she had been. It had taken her many weeks to realise there were no earnings. There was only debt.

She never saw the black book again and she had never been paid. There was one man who came sometimes, he was older, wore a suit with a tie and he liked Luca to watch him. Before he left, he always gave her a blue note with the number five on it. When he gave her the money, her heart would beat so fast – Girls will not take money from customer – and each time before going back to the waiting room, she ran to the bathroom and flushed the note down the toilet.

She remembered once, in Mrs Smith's English lesson, seeing a photograph of an English note – Look children, great British pound! But the blue note with the number five was the closest she ever came to seeing English money.

So tonight I will take you for some fun, Romolo said, as he watched her putting on the new earrings. She shook her head gently and watched the light catch the golden droplets. We will dance, drink, you will meet some of my people.

Fun. It was a strange word. Luca could not remember anyone ever telling her that she was about to have fun before. Her mother had never said, Come on, I will take you to the shops, it will be fun! Her father had never said, Luca! I will take you to the park, let's have some fun! It was a bourgeois ideal, fun, for rich people who did not have more important things to do with their lives. And here she was, Luca, new sparkling earrings, clean soft hair around her naked shoulders, a miniskirt showing off her bare legs, about to go disco dancing. They would have to drive a long way to find this fun, but Romolo did not seem to mind.

Romolo drove his car slowly around the outside of the discotheque and Luca saw a long line of people waiting outside the building. They were wrapped in coats and scarves, stamping, clapping hands, holding each other, kissing to pass the time, waiting to be let in.

For a moment, Luca worried that she had not brought a coat with her – she had nothing smart enough to wear over her outfit – but there was nothing to worry about. As they approached the entrance, two big men unhooked the ropes and let them pass. One of them nodded to Romolo as they entered. The moment she was inside, Luca felt the thud of the music in her chest and the heat of so many bodies in once place. They walked past a long bar area where people were waving money and shouting orders at barmen above the noise of the music. There were green lights, brilliant white lights that flashed, smoke rising from a platform in the middle and a dance floor larger than the factory floor. Romolo held her hand as they walked up a dark staircase. At the top there was a door with the letters VIP in silver. As they entered this room, it was like they were in a different place. The music was softer; more tune, less beat. There were sofas, glass tables, a long shiny black bar and waitresses in sexy outfits delivering bottles and glasses from round trays they held in one hand. A man stood and waved Romolo over to a booth where a group of people were sitting. Luca recognised some of the men that Romolo introduced her to, boys from school, no longer boys; now men in suits with beautiful women in their arms or on their laps and their wallets full of lei and dollar notes.

On the table was a large bottle of Russian vodka, a bucket of ice and tall glasses waiting to be filled. Luca and Romolo sat down with the others and he kept his arm around her shoulder as he poured from the bottle to the glass. When he drank, he passed the glass in front of her face so that icy drips fell onto her chest. Romolo was right, Luca thought to herself. This is fun. Tonight I feel like a movie star.

As they danced, she watched herself in the mirrors that surrounded the walls. She was young, tall, slim, her legs were strong, her hair was thick and her breasts were high. You will never look better than this, Luca, she thought to herself. In the mirror, she saw Romolo reach an arm out for her and pull her close to him as the music slowed.

She slept on the journey home. Warm car, street lights passing in a line of hazy colour.

They were at the bottom of the hill when he pulled the car onto the dark edge of the road. It was late, or early, she was not sure which.

Get into the back of the car.

She rubbed her eyes. Why? But she realised as she said it that it was a stupid question. Not here. Not now… she said.

He looked at her, made no move towards her.

Someone might see – my house is only on the hill. What if…

He leant over her and pushed the door open. I have to go away for business.

The cold air burst into the car.

She wondered what she would do if he gave her another chance right now. Would she do what he asked or would she risk making him so cross again? She wanted to kiss him, feel his soft stubble on her neck, warm hands count her ribs. She wanted to stay in the comfort of his car with the scent and the spice and the leather and the music.

He looked straight ahead.

She got out of the car and he leant over the passenger seat, took the door handle from the inside and pulled the door towards him. It slammed and he accelerated into the darkness, red lights disappearing into the night. She stood on the side of the road, half a mile from her home.

As she began to walk up the hill, the wind reached into her top and stiffened her fingers. She would be grateful for her coat now, no matter that it was old-fashioned, second-hand and did not look nice with her outfit. Seven minutes ago her life had been perfect. Now she was not sure it would ever be right again.

★★★

The man with the green coat continued.

Girls must keep the customer happy.

He took her neck between his hands.

Girls will cover up bruises, bites, scratches.

She felt the stubble from his face on her.

She wanted to ask him to stop.

Girls will not talk to customer or complain.

★★★

She was outside the church holding her little sister's hand when she saw Romolo. She had not seen him for over a week.

Little Sparrow! Have you been avoiding me? Romolo said, as he got out of the car and walked towards them. Her sister's small fingers tightened around hers as he approached.

He took out a bar of chocolate and bent over to give it to Irina and, whilst she opened it, he stood up to look at Luca.

So, what did you pray for today?

Many things, she said.

Did you pray for Romolo to come back to you? he asked quietly, moving closer to her.

His dark hair gleamed in the winter light, his long jeans fell below the heels of his cowboy boots, and his shirt, black with purple swirls, peeped through the lapels of his leather jacket. She imagined these were the clothes people from foreign cities wore, where fashion mattered and people had money to buy such things. And she inhaled the smell, the leathery spicy scent that filled her with warmth. There was no one like Romolo in Zirsk. In future, she thought, I must treat him more carefully.

Well, he asked, did you pray for me?

Maybe, Luca answered, and she smiled at him.

★★★

She cleaned up after the man with the green coat and went straight to the sleeproom. She opened the make-up box the girls shared. A shoe-box full of sticky colours and matted brushes.

Girls will cover up bruises, bites, scratches.

★★★

Luca made love to Romolo in his car. Engine running, songs playing. But she had said no when he told her he wanted to watch from the front whilst a friend joined her in the back. A nice friend, you will like him, a pretty boy but not much experience.

No, she said, I cannot do that. And when she said it, she knew he would be cross with her, but she did not know how cross.

At first she was relieved when he disappeared again, but as the days passed and he did not drive to meet her at the bottom of the hill or he did not wait for her at the store to pay for her food or he did not take her to the bar and buy her drinks, show her off, make her laugh, life soon began to lose the glitter that he had brought.

In less than a month, Romolo had changed all their lives. Her father had begun to sleep in the bed with her mother again, even his bad leg began to look not so bad. Irina began to disco dance in the kitchen to imaginary music and her brother had asked a girl to come home from school with him one day. A study afternoon he called it and they ate biscuits and drank water together whilst looking at a school textbook. Her mother began to wear an almost-smile on her face every day now and, best of all, Luca loved the mornings they shared.

She had not spent time with her mother for many years, time where her mother was not dissatisfied with Luca for something. But now, before the rest of the family got up, before it was light even, Luca and her mother made breakfast together, neither woman talking, just working. Luca prepared wood and lit the fire whilst her mother poured water into a pan and placed it on the hot stove. Mostly sleepy from a late night, Luca did not mind because her mother had the almost-smile and she seemed pleased with Luca.

There was a feeling that came to her though, sometimes. It was the feeling that she had forgotten to do something important and could not remember what it was, but if she did not do it then something would go wrong. Then one morning the feeling grew into something she could almost touch. With Romolo in her life, she had less time for God. God will understand, she thought. He knows how things are. But Luca felt the guilt when her mother was preparing to go to evening prayers with Irina and Tomas whilst she was putting on lipstick and high heels.

Go, Luca, her mother said. I can pray for both of us. But having someone else say your prayers felt like cheating.

With Romolo away – for how long, she did not know – Luca went early one morning to make her peace. As she pushed the heavy oak door, she entered alone into the cool, dark quiet of the church.

The smell of candle wax, the dusty wood.

Her feet made no noise as she approached the altar. She crossed herself in front of the Holy Mother and then took a new candle. She held its wick over a burning flame and set it alight. She watched the fire burn for a moment; the tiny orange flame flickered and behind it glittered the gold and gilt of the beloved Mother. All the candles burnt together, some nearly reaching the end of their wick, others, like hers, freshly lit. Their wax slid slowly into the sand below and Luca thought for a moment that she saw something else – a pattern emerge.

She blinked and turned silently, taking her place in the first row, on her knees, head bowed, hands together, eyes closed.

She would usually say morning prayers at this time of day, but her need was greater right now. She needed to confirm her faith and her relationship with God. As she spoke, it was softly into her hands, her thumbs touching her nose. The words did not come from a book or a sheet but from her mind and from her heart.

I believe in one God, she whispered. One God, she said again, then waited a moment before she continued. The Father Almighty, maker of heaven and earth and of all things visible and invisible. And in the Lord Jesus Christ, the Son of God, light of light, true God of true God, begotten, not made, of one essence with the Father, by whom all things were made… And He was crucified for us…and suffered, and was buried. And the third day He arose again…and ascended into heaven, and sits at the right hand of the Father… and He shall come again with glory to judge the living and the dead; Whose Kingdom shall have no end…

She said her amen, crossed herself and looked at the Virgin Mother. She felt that God would not mind her adding a personal prayer.

Perhaps I will have to do something in return if I ask you this, she said almost silently, just her lips moving. Perhaps I am not in a position to bargain with you. But if there is a bargain to be made, I would like to make it.

She closed her eyes and said aloud, Please bring him back.

That afternoon, she made the long walk to the factory, brown dirt and grit now turned to ice as she trod carefully on the road that had not yet been built.

Anything today?

Soon.

How soon?

Try again next week.

★★★

When Luca took her chair in the waiting room, Madame looked at her, then at her watch, then back to the open book on her desk.

Punishments came unexpectedly. They arrived sometimes days after the crime. Today Luca's crime might be: Taking too long to come to waiting room after job. Punishments were never the same. Sometimes punishments were fatal. Luca lived in fear of doing anything that might bring punishment.

Her name was called.

Behind her, lots of little steps like a bird hopping along a windowsill. The rub of corduroy on corduroy, the smell of curry spices, cloves, hair oil, a door closed gently. Apologetically? Soft hands, a fleshy stomach, wet lips.

Luca closed her eyes and she tried to remember the story. The Prince, the stallion, riding over the wasteland to the Green Emperor's palace. As a child she pulled the cover closer to herself and felt the horror of what was to come. It was a terrible forest. So dark, so many trees, so many paths. There was no way for the horse to fly up and there was no light to guide them onwards. They turned many circles, always returning to the same spot. There was nothing to eat, just the red berries that fell from the wide tree, but the berries burnt them. All the time, hungrier, thirstier, weaker.

He came three times – Spanul, the Bald Man, the evil creature that was trapped in the forest. Her mother never described him. Luca asked, What does he look like? How should I know? her mother would say. He looks evil. But what does evil look like? Luca would ask, but her mother would go on with the story. If she described him just once, it would have been better, there would have been something to attach her fear to, a picture. But with no description, her fear grew with each image her mind created.

When Spanul trapped the Prince, he forced him into slavery, stole his identity and gave him the name Harap Alb. When they arrived at the emperor's palace they were master and servant, Spanul the master, Harap Alb, the slave.

The Bald Man was so cruel to him. He beat him and sent him into the forest to show the emperor what a clever and strong master he was. The first time, Harap had to bring back the Lettuce of the Bear and on the second he had to kill and bring back the Jewelled Stag's head. It was only because the old beggar woman, Holy Sunday, came back to him that Harap was able to return to the palace alive. But the worst challenge was still to come. The Bald Man sent him on an impossible task – to trap the Red Emperor's daughter, said to be a dark witch – and bring her back so they could put her on trial.

Luca could not wait for Holy Sunday to appear to the Prince again. It seemed too much to ask one young man to do alone and she pictured Holy Sunday as she waited for him in the forest, a light amongst the trees.

Luca opened her eyes and the man was gone, the door closed quietly behind him.

Luca wanted to get back to the waiting room quickly. If she was very quick perhaps Madame would forget how long it took her to clean up after the man in the green coat. Tanya was coming towards her and Luca walked close to the wall but there was nowhere left to go and Tanya's shoulder jammed hard into hers.

Clumsy.

Luca said nothing.

I said, Clumsy. Watch where you are going.

Luca tried to step past her, she needed to get back to the waiting room quickly.

Where are you going in such a hurry? Looking for Loverboy? Why don't you answer? You afraid?

Her breast pressed on Luca's shoulder as she whispered in her ear. There is no Loverboy, Luca. Romolo will want me to be the next Madame, not you. Poor Luca is jealous! Luca could feel her hot breath in her ear. I will have topjob, Luca. Travel in smart suit back to Moldova, Russia, Romania, recruiting for new girls. Not you. You will work for me and if you think the job is bad now then wait until Tanya is in charge.

Luca's other shoulder was up against the wall and Tanya's face was next to hers. The wall was cold on her bare flesh, flakes of plaster scratched at her skin and Tanya was so close she could smell the stale scent of lipstick grease. The two women stood like this for several moments until Luca swung away from the wall to move off.

Yes, walk away now. But soon there will be no walking away from me, Luca.

Luca glanced at the seats before she sat on a brown chair. Still no Natalie. She kept her head bowed but she knew Madame was looking at her.

She heard footsteps come into the room and, with her head still down, she was able to see a pair of shoes. Shiny shoes that had once been white, a metal buckle at the ankle, high heels, small feet. Olya? Perhaps Tatyana? She did not dare to check.

She did not know how many people there were in the house. Sometimes she would see a face, then never see it again. It was three weeks before she found out that she shared the sleeproom with seven other girls. She knew they existed because of the traces left behind: cheap body spray, the scent of the green and white soap from the bathroom, the slicing smell of nail polish, men. No matter how hard they washed, always the smell of men.

They left clothes rolled, folded, spread out, crumpled – each girl her own way of leaving a mark – but the clothes were not their own. There was a box, and every day they had to pick something to wear. Sometimes the box was taken away and a new one put in its place, but the clothes were always the same: Hotpants, shortskirt, boobtube, lacetop, babydoll.

If they saw each other, they kept their heads down. No one

wanted to look for trouble. But one night Luca was woken by tears and she could not stop herself from going closer to the girl and, one by one, the other girls also came. They came together in a tiny space, to comfort the girl who could not hold her tears in any longer. They sat on the floor, cross-legged, eyes becoming accustomed to the dark, not daring to put a light on – Girls will not speak to each other – and they whispered.

I am Luca, this is Natalie.

I am Tatyana.

I am Ludmila.

I am Raisa.

I am Yana.

I am sorry that I woke you with my crying. I am Olya. I am sixteen years old and I miss my family.

Tanya stayed in the corner of the room, but Luca knew she was listening. She lit a cigarette and kept her ear towards them. Luca could tell she was as hungry for this contact as they were.

Each girl told the same story of the same journey and the same faces, but they moved away from these stories quickly – they wanted to spend the little time they had together sharing the parts of themselves they remembered before this.

Do you miss bread pudding? My mother made the best and my father would always notice when we took his whiskey for the sauce… Yes, Zirsk, I know it. Do you know Svetlana Movoro? Yes! We were at school together when we were small – the last time I saw her she told me she was going to be an internet bride! Do you remember the snow we had that year? Yes, it was terrible but we were so cosy in bed!

As they talked, Luca kept thinking to herself, All of these things from home were tired, sad, broken. I was so unhappy with everything in my life. Looking for work every day was so hard. My only dream was to escape and find a new life in a new city with new people, but now I speak about that life and I miss it. I want it back. If I could have it back, I would never ask for anything again.

Luca watched Natalie. Her friend sat with her hands in her lap, away from the group, looking at the door. Come, she whispered to her. Join in. We need this. But Natalie pulled her hand away and would not take her eyes from the door.

They did not sleep until shafts of light came through the boarded-up window. Each girl drifted back to her own space in the room and after that night there had not been another time when they came together. They saw each other in the waiting room, passed each other in the hallway, heard each other in the workroom and felt traces of each other as they moved around the house, silently, from one job to the next.

Today I get credit, Luca's mother said, with the almost-smile on her face. Today old Dinu takes me to the front of the line. What can we do for you, Madam Tasca? Have you seen fine cured ham for sale? Would you like to feel how fresh are tomatoes today? Ha! Now they want business from me. Now my daughter has a job offer from overseas.

Not exactly a job offer, Mama. Romolo says his company will find me a good waitress job in Italy. We must go there first for interviews.

Interview. Job. All the same thing. She put the bags on the table and walked over to Luca. She took her face in her hands and Luca could feel the roughred skin on her cheeks. She saw only the woman she was now, the drooping eyelids, sagging cheeks, stubby lashes and she thought to herself, A woman does not stay beautiful for long, not in a hard place like Zirsk with freezing winters and factory work or, worse still, no work.

Her mother stood back. My daughter. A waitress overseas.

She smiled. It was not an almost-smile, it was a full smile, stained teeth, lips cracking as they pulled into a new shape.

She clapped her hands once, loudly. Now. We cook for this man who brings us good fortune. Empty the bag, Luca, we must work.

She opened the cupboard and took her apron from a nail on the back of the door. She put it on, smoothed it over her body, began to arrange knives, spoons, sieves. There was a feeling of celebration, Christmas maybe, and she talked to herself as she cooked, instructing herself on what to do. So, we put this here, some of this in here, a bit of this there. Yes. Good.

Luca emptied the bag onto the kitchen table and arranged everything in piles. Tomatoes, onions, cabbage, beetroot, potatoes, garlic, carrot. A leg of ham, a small chicken.

Luca looked at the chicken. The bird's eyes were closed, goosebump skin like she was cold without her feathers, her toes curled up as if she had been holding on to her perch at the moment she had been killed, wanting to stay in that warm safe place. Luca wondered whether she had she been miserable in her cage. Did she know what it was like to live a free chicken life and raise her own babies and flap her wings in the sunshine? These things made Luca sad, but there was no place for sadness in their home right now.

Her mother took hold of the chicken's legs and pulled them apart, put her hand inside and removed the guts.

Skinny bird. No good for roasting but it will make good soup, she said. Luca picked up her knife, took hold of a carrot and began to chop.

The ham sat in the oven covered in spices and glaze for six hours, the chicken soup simmered for two hours, the vegetables were scrubbed with an old brush over the sink, chopped, diced, boiled and thrown into the soup. No, it was not like Christmas; they had never had a Christmas like this before.

Irina and Tomas were drawn into the kitchen by the smells

and the activity but they were shooed away by their mother. Leave this work to the women! Go! she said with her new smile. From now on, with the money you send, Luca, we will eat like this every Sunday. Cold ham on Monday and Tuesday, chicken soup for the rest of the week, always fresh vegetables for borsch. She looked at her daughter. Then, when the work is done, you will come home, maybe have a family of your own.

Will I come home? wondered Luca and she also wondered how she would be dressed for work. A waitress outfit would be black, with a white apron, shiny shoes, hair tied back, copper lipstick. But whatever she wore, she would work hard. She would work hard and she would not disappoint Romolo.

The children were clean and dressed in smart clothes, her mother wore her new scarf, Luca the blouse and her father sat at the table with a clean shirt over his vest. When he tried to eat the food, his wife brushed his hand away. We will wait for our guest.

By the time Romolo arrived, it was nearly 10 o'clock.

He looked surprised to see the table set with food and plates and cups and knives and forks and he looked like he might leave straight away.

Please, join us for this humble meal, said Luca's mother, as he waited by the door. We ask that you look after our daughter and bring her home safely to us. Her mother's smile had gone and her green eyes looked at Romolo. One hand she extended to him, the other to the table.

It amused Luca to see that Romolo was trapped. Trapped by her mother's good intentions and a table full of food.

They all sat down for supper.

Romolo forked food onto his plate and ate quickly. Big mouthfuls, strong jaws working the food in his mouth. At first there was no conversation, but after the food began to settle in his belly Romolo began to talk as he ate, using his fork to gesticulate the way he would with his hands.

So, he said, tonight we must leave. And he looked at Luca. The agency is desperate. There is a new hotel, desperate for beautiful girls to work as waitresses. We must get there before all the good jobs go.

But I have not packed yet… Luca began to say. Then she stopped. Romolo gave her that look he had given her before and each time he had given her that look, he disappeared – each time longer than the last. No, she could not let him leave now. But it will not take me long. I do not have so much to pack, she said.

She served her bread pudding with whiskey sauce. As she ate, it stuck to the roof of her mouth. More sauce just made it tacky on her tongue. It has been left too long and it has dried out, she thought. I wanted him to know how well I can cook. Every man wants a wife who can fill his belly well.

Romolo left, promising to return for Luca in one hour and whilst he was gone her father sat at the table sucking his teeth clean as Luca and her mother tried to find a bag to put Luca's things in.

I do not like the man, he said. Make sure you get a good payment first, Luca. Never trust a young man with money. I see now they like to think they are big gangsters!

Petru! said her mother. Do not say this. He has given Luca an incredible opportunity and now she will earn money to look after the whole family. No matter that he is young. He has work for Luca. That is good enough for me!

Madame left the waiting room to answer her cell phone again and Luca felt the breeze from the door as it shut. There had been no visitors for about thirty minutes, which was unusual because there were always visitors, they came all day, at breakfast, midnight – there was no timetable for visitors' needs.

Madame stood in front of them with her cell phone still in her hand. Tonight we have a special treat, she said. I think all girls here would like to be a waitress, no? With nice uniform, no? All girls will go downstairs now and wait for collection. There is a special new job for all girls.

None of the girls looked at each other as they began to stand and leave the room and Luca suddenly thought of her friend upstairs.

You, Madame said to Luca. You bring lazy girl from the sleeproom. Be quick.

Luca left through the same door and walked along the hall. No footsteps behind her. Alone for a few moments. She stopped and looked over her shoulder and she turned to walk faster. Never alone, even when alone. Always the feeling someone was watching and following. Up the stairs. High steps, narrow walls, darkness. She counted them, seven, eight, nine, ten, eleven. She passed the bathroom, saw the shower curtain pulled across the bath, the bucket they used for a basin, the window, one pane still broken, letting in the English winter.

She had looked out the window many times – Girls will be quick in washroom – and had seen the street below. The grey road, a proper road, with grass growing along each side. Houses joined together in a straight line, red brick, white painted window frames, curtains she could almost see through, always closed. Twice she had seen a woman leaving the house opposite, both times she had been pushing a pram and had a small girl next to her. Each time she locked the door, put her keys in her bag and walked out of the gate and away from the house whilst talking to the child. Once she reached into the pram to do something with the baby. Luca wanted to see the baby so much, but both times the baby had been facing away from her.

There was not always time to look out of the window, but Luca held on to the things she saw and knew of the country she now lived in. It was a real place, with real people in it. This house was not a world, it was not real, it was just a house. The people out there, did they know what happened in this house? Did they ever see men come and go and think about what must happen here? Did they know what happened in their road? Perhaps, thought Luca, this is what English people expect.

Natalie was still lying on her side, arms wrapped around herself. She was on the floor with a coat over her.

Can you get up? Natalie did not answer. Heavy breath came from a place deep inside her. Eyes shut. Face swollen. Leg still turned out, horrible angle away from the knee.

★★★

Little Sparrow, sleep, we have a long journey. Romolo had given her a small bottle of vodka. Drink, more, yes, good girl. He was in a nice mood; Luca felt safe.

She lay on the back seat of his car, warm, sleepy, the vodka had made her very sleepy.

Zirsk, thirty minutes behind them. Old life, new life.

Her mother had cried, roughred hands to her face.

Her father had said, Do not forget to send money. Do not spend it on the high-life in Italy.

When she got into the back seat of the car, she had looked at the house. Snow was stacked on the widows, the small flicker of an early-morning candle shining through the glass. The orange flame made the house look warm on the inside, but Luca knew it was only a trick of the eye. Without her father working, it was going to be a long winter and there would be much hunger in the house.

Romolo turned the music up as they drove away from Zirsk.

We are stopping to pick up a friend for the journey, he said over the tune. Nothing to worry about, sleep Little Sparrow.

The warmth of the car, the feel of the road underneath her, the vodka hot in her stomach.

Oh, I nearly forgot. Give me your passport. Good girl. This way, you can sleep whilst Romolo does all the work.

Perhaps she dreamt as she slept, or maybe not. She heard voices. Men's voices, girls' voices, then no voices, just the feeling of other bodies in the car with her, next to her on the back seat. Then Romolo's reassuring voice. Sleep, Little Sparrow, sleep.

So warm, so sleepy.

Old life, new life.

★★★

A room, dark. A smell, damp. No window.

Cold. Hands to flesh, no clothes. Naked in a bed.

Head, thick. Unable to think. Sick. No light.

She gets up from the bed, arms in front of her, eyes wide trying to see. No door.

The feel of rough bricks on her palms. She vomits.

Hot fluid splashes up from the floor on her legs. Cold, shivering. Darkness.

She gets back on the bed. No sheet.

She sits up, knees to her – covering herself in the darkness.

Time passes.

How much time?

Who can say in the darkness?

In the cold.

On the bed with no sheet.

Maybe hours.

Maybe days.

Does she sleep?

She does not know.

Who can tell?

Who can say in the darkness?

In the cold.

On the bed with no sheet.

Then she hears footsteps. Metal on concrete, long strides.

Feet that strike hard on the floor.

Then someone comes in.

★★★

Luca looked to the door again. She could not stay much longer with Natalie.

She thought of her, before all this, sitting on the wall outside her house in her school uniform, legs kicking against the bricks, lace-up shoes passed down from her sister, waiting for Luca. Their walk to school. Their plans, always their plans of a grown-up life. I will do this, you must live there, we will have this, we will be this.

But they had never thought of this.

She imagined Natalie's mother in Dinu's shop, with her account running. An account with imported ham, bottles of beer, feel-how-fresh-they-are tomatoes, chicken with eyes rolled back, beak closed, legs tied together, claws curled tight. And she wondered how long it took Dinu to stop her account. How long it would take him to stop her mother's account, and she wondered if her father said, You see, Maria? I told you. She is spending money on the high-life in Italy, or whether he said, Where is Luca? Why have we not heard from her? We should check with police to see if there is a problem.

Luca listened. There was a car pulling up outside the house. Easy to hear such things on a nice quiet road. Then another car came and she heard doors open, girls getting in, engine still running, high heels on concrete.

Then she heard footsteps.

Metal on concrete.

Long strides. Feet that struck hard on the floor.

There was a minute of silence, only the noise of the engine running and Madame's voice, high and sharp in the background.

She looked to the door, felt a breeze as it opened and, then, he came in.

★★★

Romolo holds her tightly. He rocks her. The smell of him, leather spices, warm, clean, satin shirt on her cheek. Poor Little Sparrow, poor Little Sparrow. She cries. She holds on to him. I have a friend coming. He wants to see you. I do not like this man. He is a bad man. You must please him, okay, Little Sparrow? You must please him. Poor Little Sparrow. He stands up and she can see him in the light that comes from the door. Do you have to go? Can you stay? No, Little Sparrow, this man is coming, you see. Be a good girl and it will all be okay.

Time passes. How much time?

Who can tell in this cold, dark damp. Alone, naked, cold. No toilet, a corner, a bucket, no water, a tray with a drink that always burns the throat.

She hears footsteps coming. Running shoes on concrete. A nylon coat that rubs at the sleeves. A bald man stands in the doorway. Short, wide arms that stand away from the side of his body. He wears big rings on big fingers. His neck is thick.

He carries something in his hand.

★★★

For those few moments that she spent alone with Natalie, Luca held her friend's hand. If only there were something she could say that would bring life into Natalie's eyes, would make her think of another place, something that was not this room, these people.

Do you remember the story of Harap Alb, Natalie? she asked her friend. I think about that story when I do not want to think about what is happening here. I remember every piece of the story and the way my mother used to tell it to me. You remember when Holy Sunday helped the Prince capture the Jewelled Stag? Luca lay down beside her friend and stroked her hair as she spoke in an end-of-day voice, the sort of voice her own mother had used with her when she had been small.

I was so frightened in the part where he was waiting for the stag to die. He lay in the dark pit all night and put his hands over his ears – that stag called out to him in a human voice, asking for mercy and Harap would have gone, but Holy Sunday stopped him because the stag wanted to look at him with his poison eye.

She could hear Natalie's breath, faint, but there.

You must remember the last challenge to bring back the Red Emperor's daughter? They said she was a dark witch, but when Harap found her she was sad and beautiful and lonely and wanted to go with him. His friends helped him to get home through the forest – do you remember what we used to say? Gerila, who could turn anything to ice with his breath, was like Mr Zolozi from the bar because of the mints he used to eat; Flamanzila, who could eat anything and never be full, was like Greta at school who was so fat; Setila, who could drink everything, was like your father because he loved his vodka so much; Ochila, who could see so far, was like Madam Voski from the house opposite who always watched us playing and Pasari-Lati-Lungilla, who could grow to fit any space – who did we say he was like? I cannot remember now. She paused for a moment waiting perhaps for Natalie to say something, then she went on: But how wonderful; they fell in love on the way back. Luca stopped talking then. She did not remind Natalie of the part where the Bald Man had been waiting for them at the palace with a sword in his hand.

★★★

Poor Little Sparrow. So terrible. This bad man. He has taken pictures. It is terrible. He wants to send them to your family, but I say no. Pictures are revolting. They do not look like my Luca I tell him. Look at this one – he shows it to Luca. She looks away. And this one, he makes a sound through his teeth, takes her face, makes her look at it. So I tell him, Luca is a good girl, she will do as you say. You do not have to do this thing. And do you know what he says? He tells me if you try to get away from him he will kill your mother and what is the name of your little sister? Ah, yes, Irina, he will kill her too, but first he says he will bring her here to see if she is good merchandise. So terrible. He looks through the pictures. Disgusting. This is not my Luca. And I tell him, there is no need to kill poor mother and sister – what have they done? Luca is a good girl. She will do as you say. And he tells me he needs to make sure. Poor Little Sparrow. He needs to make sure. He holds her tight. He rocks her. He smells so clean. How long has she been here? When did she last wash? Is she in Italy yet? Who can tell in the dark? Alone, cold, naked, the drink that burns.

She hears footsteps coming. Running shoes on concrete. A nylon coat that rubs at the sleeves. She crawls to the corner of the room. Concrete scraping her knees. She hides her face behind her hands, pulls her knees to herself, feels the rough brick of the walls press hard against her body.

She hears the voice.

I will ask you again, Luca, he says. I will ask you again, but only one more time. Who is your God, Luca?

She cannot speak. The voice gets closer.

No more times, Luca. Who is your God?

It is hard for her to move her mouth. You. She does not know her own voice.

Who is your God, Luca? The voice so close. She wants it to go. To leave her alone. She must say it.

You. You are my God, Mikhail.

Yes. The voice is on top of her now and she shuts her eyes tight. Yes, he says. Mikhail is your God now, Luca.

★★★

The van was dark except for a finger of light which came through where the rear doors met. The doors rattled and the light came and went with each turn. Luca sat opposite Tanya and she watched her, making up a picture of her as each new light shone into the van. Arms crossed, leaning back, dark eyes. Dark eyes like a shark, Luca had once thought, but now they were dark eyes with something else in them. Her hair was scraped back from her face and the deep space at the base of her throat was moving quickly up and down. If I did not know her so well, thought Luca, I would think she is trying to stop the tears from coming. But then Tanya leant forwards and grabbed Luca's arm, pulling it towards her. Darkness fell around them as the van turned and Luca felt the other girl's hand, hot on her skin.

You saw Loverboy, prettygirl Luca?

Luca tried to pull her arm away.

And what did he tell you? You have brightfuture?

Luca could feel the other girls trying to shuffle along the seat away from them, leaving a space between themselves and the trouble they could see was coming.

Did he tell you to listen to Tanya because soon all girls will answer to Tanya? She held her arm tight, the tips of her nails denting Luca's skin. What did he say to you?

Luca looked at Tanya and could see that yes, her eyes were full of almost-tears. Almost-tears collecting in the middle of her eyes – if they ran out they would fall down to the point of her nose and into her mouth, but her lips were tight shut and her face was fierce. She wants to know what Romolo said to me, she thought, but for the first time Romolo did not say anything.

He listened. He had listened to Luca when he found her sitting beside Natalie, telling the story of Harap. He had listened as she turned from her friend and spoke to him. Then both of them had looked up, guilty, as Madame Povrovski came in, apologising to Romolo, Terrible behaviour! Girls will not do these things again. She looked at Natalie, I will not allow these disruptions to work, and then she pushed Luca with a hard finger, out of the sleeproom, down the stairs, past the workroom, away from the waiting room.

Luca did not see where Romolo went as she was pushed into the back of the van, onto the bench seat opposite Tanya.

He did not say anything, Luca said to Tanya.

The van bumped over the road, the doors swung and more light came through.

The van stopped and the floorboards shook with the idling motion of the engine. Luca felt it move up from her feet into her knees, into her thighs. The van moved off quickly and the girls were thrown together at the back of the bench seat – sweat, grease, perfume, stale clothes, the smell of men, always the smell of men – and Tanya, still holding her, looking at her from across the van. As Luca began to shake her arm to release herself, the van turned, the doors rattled and the back of the van filled with light, a false light from the street. One door swung open and the girls could see the world beyond their own. There was silence. Nobody moved. It was as if the van was a cage and the girls were birds in a pet shop. The cage was all they knew, so when the door opened they did not fly away. They sat bunched on the seat as if tied together and Luca did not think of Natalie or her mother or her father or her brother or her sister or the factory or Romolo or the Bald Man or what would be on the other side of the van door as she jumped.

She fell onto the tarmac. It was wet and hard underneath her and she felt a weight on top of her and she felt Tanya's grip, still tight on her arm. The exhaust coughed petrol and fumes over them and the smell of rubber tyres were strong in her nose. The girls lay very still as the van moved off and Luca wondered if it was a trick, if they would be collected by Madame who was watching them and they were about to receive a punishment they would never forget.

She watched as the van disappeared into the darkness. The door banged shut and she could no longer see any of the girls inside. Tatyana whose favourite food was clatite and had dreamed of owning her own pancake restaurant one day, Ludmila who had wanted to be a dancer since she had seen *Flashdance* when she was five, Raisa who had hoped one day she would have seven children, Yana who cared for her sick mother until she died when Yana was just thirteen years old, and Olya who was sixteen years old and had woken them all up with her crying that night because she missed her family and her home – Luca had never learnt the rest of their names, maybe ten of them or more. The faces she passed in the hallway, feet she saw in the waiting room, the traces she had noticed in the sleeproom, the lives she knew nothing about. Those girls were swallowed up in the dark van and taken into the night.

Tanya held onto Luca and the two girls lay on the ground, still waiting, perhaps for someone to claim them or tell them what to do next. But the night was still.

A proper road, with a pavement at each side, trees growing out of the concrete, a cat, eyes bright in the dark, scratching at the tree bark, straight white lines painted in the middle of the road.

Luca twisted her arm out of Tanya's grip, took the taller girl's hand, pulled her up and began to run. She ran as far as she could and as fast as she could in high-heeled shoes. Past the tree-lined road, into other roads that looked exactly the same, through an alley with high walls at either side and across a road with loud music coming from an open door. Their feet echoed over the river footbridge, then dulled as they hit the edge of the canal. They kept running along the water's edge until they came to a cobbled street that led them onto a big road with two lanes of cars going in each direction. Buses with lights on, cars with headlights, restaurants with people inside, overhead streetlights. The contrast between night and day was so great that Luca felt confused. She had never seen so much light when it should be dark.

It was only when she stopped running that she noticed the chill night air coating the inside of her throat and chest and she began to cough and swallow, trying to wet her throat and warm it from the inside.

Tanya turned to Luca and spoke for the first time through deep breaths. What now, prettygirl Luca? she said. Romolo was going to give me topjob. What now?

Luca pulled her hand away from Tanya's. There is no topjob, Tanya. Just bodies.

And Luca remembered those few moments she'd had with Romolo in the sleeproom. She hoped Natalie had heard what she said to him because since Luca arrived, Natalie had not been able to live with what she had done.

I gave him your name, Luca, she said on the first night they discovered each other in the house, their voices urgent whispers in the dark. I told him you were pretty, would be a good worker. He said he had a special opportunity for a good friend of mine… I thought… he was so kind, so handsome… Luca told her that she knew no one refused Romolo and it was okay, she understood, but still, each day Natalie got worse. She stopped eating, stopped drinking, stopped talking and it had seemed to Luca that she stopped breathing. There was nothing Luca could do for her until, finally, two days ago, the jump from the tiny bathroom window from an upside-down bucket. Her friend fell, twisted on the street below, not dead but such horrible injuries. Natalie had been alone, had wanted to end her life, had made the jump, had almost died, whilst Luca was being fucked in the room underneath.

Luca hoped that Natalie could hear what she said to Romolo.

The noise of the engines running outside, the sound of Madame's voice, the thought that perhaps Natalie did not have long left to live made her talk fast and made her say things she did not think she would ever dare to say. Romolo stood silently as she spoke.

Why this? she asked him. Why *this*?

I knew there was never going to be a waitress job in Italy. I knew that. I am not as stupid as you think. I knew you would bring me to something like a prostitute's job. But I did not care because I thought you would look after me. I could show you what a good worker I was, I could earn money, send it to my family. You look surprised that I am not so stupid after all, but when I met you, all the time I was thinking, What does Luca have over all the pretty girls in Zirsk, in Moldova? What does Luca have that they do not? What does Luca have that Romolo wants? Only this. She grabbed her own breasts in her hands, cupped them from underneath and thrust them forwards, the red Lycra ruching over her skin. I have a body; a body can make money. You see. I know all this. I expect this, but I thought you would look after me, it would not be so bad, two years maybe and done. Home, money. But this! Why this? Why you do *this*? Her hands were still on her breasts when Madame Povrovski walked in.

Romolo had not spoken, but she knew that he had heard her.

Natalie had not moved, but she felt sure her friend had heard her too.

As Madame Povrovski pushed Luca out of the room, she realised that she had not finished telling Natalie the story. But surely she would remember Harap Alb's marriage to the Red Emperor's daughter? Surely she would remember the game they used to play when they pretended to be guests at the never-ending-wedding-feast and how they had imagined they were dressed in feathers and bows and soft silk as they ate the finest food and drank delicious cherry brandy and danced with the most handsome and richest princes in the room and how the music never stopped playing and they never stopped dancing until it was time to begin the feast all over again.

She looked at Tanya now, same girl but different outside on this road, with the English winter all over her.

There is no topjob for girls like us, Tanya, said Luca. She turned away from the girl and looked back only once to see her with her arms by her side, legs long and bare, her face pale and her eyes dark. Within seconds she was hidden behind the cars, trucks, smoke and noise of the city at night.

Luca crossed the road, walked under a narrow railway bridge and found herself in a square. In the centre was a fenced park and at the edges were rows of red-bricked houses attached to each other.

There was a pub on the corner with people standing outside smoking. As she passed them, the conversation quietened and Luca could hear the click of her own heels on the concrete. She kept her eyes to the ground. Again, I am wishing for my old coat, she thought. Such an old coat, such a horrible colour, but it is twice now I have wished for it.

The traffic noise from the main road was duller in the square with its trees and houses and she began to think maybe it was safer for her to be a face in a crowd of faces, but in the distance she could see a church and even though it was not the sort of church she would visit at home, she walked towards it. As she got closer, she could see its grey stone walls, the arched windows, the tower in the middle with the clock and flagpole, and by the time she was in front of it she could see the graveyard, its mossy stones wedged in the grass at different angles. She pressed her body against the gate and stared down the path that led to the dark wooden doors. The doors were closed.

There was a hazy light coming from the windows, reflecting the red and green of the glass, and Luca stood at the gate and she looked at the church for a very long time, not noticing the cold.

Finally, she took off her shoes and held them by their straps for a moment. Then she placed them tightly, side-by-side, outside the gate and she walked away from them. She walked away from the shoes, away from the church and back towards the main road where there was the noise, the traffic, the lights and the faces.

★★★

There is another girl standing in a doorway in another country. She too is waiting. In her hand the gift from last night; the soft brown bear with the red heart, so soft it makes her think of a country where nothing could be harsh or cold or rough.

She watches as the men finish their work. They pull the steel doors across the warehouse and stamp their feet as they walk away. She hears a truck engine start, then move into the distance.

There is no moon in the sky tonight, just a dim haze from the far-off lighthouse. The ships are huge on the water and the only sound comes from the ocean as it slops against the docks' edge.

He told her to wait here, but perhaps he has not seen her in the darkness. She has been waiting an hour already. She is worried she might have upset him last night. He wanted something from her and she said no, but if he asks again, she will give it to him. It is all she has to give.

She looks out of the doorway, onto the empty road and the water beyond. Dear God, she whispers, her breath steaming the night air, please make him come.

AT THE WINDOW

When I walk in she is at the window.

'Hold this will you?' she says, expecting me.

I see the dried flower arrangement first, small blooms tightly tied together. Vygies. Faded orange and dusky pink, maroon like dried blood. I can smell the dust on them.

She holds the arm out for me – a bracelet of flowers at the wrist.

'Hold this flat. Okay? Are you ready to shoot?'

The baby is sleeping and I take the arm and hold it gently against the cold pane of glass.

'She'll look nice against the light. Like an angel. You can shoot her with the light coming in behind her?'

I hold the hand, so tiny. Her eyes are closed and she's hardly dressed.

And then I realise.

The baby is dead.

I am holding her dead, cold hand against the icy glass of the window and the baby's eyes are closed because she's dead.

The mother holds her against the light.

'Are you ready?' she asks.

My camera is around my neck. I'm always ready. But now? Ready to photograph the baby against the light with the mother looking on?

She's looking right at me.

'Come on, I don't have long.'

She becomes annoyed and cradles the baby, takes her away from the cold glass and lies her on the changing mat.

'I called you and you said you could do it,' she says, as she begins to pour milk into a glass. She drinks it all down.

'I think...' I begin to say, but I don't finish the sentence.

There's a small box on the floor by the table. A candle next to it burns. That's what I smelled when I first came in. The waxy scent of honeysuckle. It's suffocating me now.

'I'll put her in here 'til you're ready.'

She gives me a look I've never seen before. Like she hates me from the inside of my soul to the split ends of my hair.

When she turns her back, I look into the box. And it sits up, looks at me with clear, green eyes.

I stumble back and grab my camera. It feels heavy around my neck.

The baby gets up, out of the box, and walks away. Through the window, the light behind it, just as the mother had wanted.

She turns and picks up the body, cradles it in her arms.

'Are you ready now?' she asks.

But I am stuck to this spot, unable to move and unable to answer.

I'm stuck in this place and I don't think I will ever move again.

ISLAND LIFE

She is the only person on the island so far this morning and she sits on her deck chair, forgetting for a moment, feeling the sun on her shoulders.

May was always her favourite time of year. It brought a crisp air and relief from the exhausting heat of high summer. She never bothered herself with the impending rains and drop in temperature before now.

Every May Michael would take her to the botanical garden's annual sale and each year Lillian made sure that she was first in line to get the best plants. Michael waited for her whilst she made her choices, then paid, usually with a grumble that she would pretend not to hear, before loading the car and driving her home.

Her ritual was always the same; she made tea then got out her garden plan which she started when they first moved in, then calculated where each new plant should live. The king protea amongst the fynbos, the wild fig alongside the bottlebrush and the red hot pokers towering out of the lily beds. When she was sure of herself, she instructed the garden boy to dig holes so that she could position the plant before he covered them over with fertiliser and soil. This was her favourite household task; placing new life into the ground and watching it rise up around the walls of her home year after year. Michael always said she could make anything grow, but she felt she owed her luck to the indigenous plants which took root in the earth, if they truly belonged there.

'Here you go, Lillian.'

She nods acknowledgement at the man who brings her breakfast most mornings. She hates the familiar tone he takes with her and never addresses him by name, hoping he will realise. As soon as he is out of sight, she bites into the roll, hungrier than she would like to be. Always hungry these days. She thought hunger abated with age. Not so for her.

Although she hasn't looked in a mirror lately, she is aware that she has lost the plump flourish of her younger years. Her clothes hang awkwardly, her hands and forearms are dotted with liver spots and she can feel wisps of unchecked hair at her cheeks. She is overdue for a salon appointment. Michael always told her never to go grey. The first strands of silver appeared at her temples during her second pregnancy and Michael drove her into town and gave her enough money for a blow dry as well as a colour treatment. She went a shade darker than her natural colour and he noticed. 'Makes you look younger,' he said as he took her elbow and weaved her through the busy Cape Town streets back to the car. His unsolicited compliment made her feel like the shy fifteen-year-old girl she had been when they first met.

She stands up, brushes the crumbs off her lap, licks her lips. She watches as the women start to arrive. Beggars with children wrapped tightly to their backs in native blankets. She knows that some of the women borrow children to increase their earning potential. She purses her lips and turns away from them before they start to hassle her and she feels obliged to move away from their hostile stares.

Michael was always firm on that point. 'See them, Lillian? The government gives them handouts to sit at home – so what they're doing here goodness only knows.' He always rolled the window up when he approached the traffic lights and looked straight ahead when beggars passed with battered, illegible signs and open hands. 'Don't even look at them, Lillian.'

She doesn't mind the slow start to her day. She slept badly last night – she sleeps badly most nights. 'Old age doesn't come alone,' her mother always said. And the old woman had been right. For Lillian it came with more than she could have imagined.

The breeze catches her nostrils. An odour that has become familiar to her. The acrid smell of human sweat, like a ripe cheese steeped in wine vinegar. If only she could get rid of that smell.

A woman settles a short distance from her. She puts her child on the ground. It seems to have just woken and is quiet with sleepy eyes. Big, watery brown eyes that stare at nothing in particular. She moves the child onto a bin bag, crumpled, split and no longer shiny black. The child sits, then curls into a foetal position, a thumb placed lightly in its mouth. The woman sits next to it, holding her sign.

She thinks about her own boys at that age and the image of those well filled out, muscular little bodies appears before her like a polaroid. They devoured everything she put in front of them and she caught them many times at the open cupboard doors, the oldest standing on a chair, the youngest sitting on the floor like a hungry chick, an accomplice to his brother's thieving ways. When they stole the Christmas cake one year and ate all the icing and decorations, she called Michael, aware that young boys could easily get out of hand without a father's firm guidance. She never sees a father begging with children. Where are all the fathers? she wonders.

She knows she should get up again, but feels dragged down by the lethargy which has been slowly overtaking her body.

She runs a finger over her cheek. Deep lines fan out from the corners of her eyes and from the base of her nose to the edge of her mouth. Being outside so much isn't good for her skin.

She always imagined that she would grow old gracefully and involuntarily looks down at herself. A single tear makes its way along the crags of her cheek. She licks the outer edge of her lip, feeling the salty liquid on her tongue. She holds an index finger to the inner corner of her eye.

She stands up on sore joints to repeat her walk. When she has finished, she returns to the deckchair and sits down. Her knee aches, her ankles are swollen, the skin mottled, reddish and yellow. She always heard that walking was good for keeping old age at bay.

Women go to the gym to keep fit these days. She sees them in their tight tracksuit trousers and bright Lycra tops and feels a slight revulsion at the amount of flesh they display. She has always walked to keep trim; gyms weren't for women when she was a young lady. After she took the children to school, she drove to Newlands Forest with her three dogs and sometimes walked for hours amongst the pines and gums. On weekends, they often went to Tokai Forest or Table Mountain Park. She packed a picnic into a rucksack for Michael to carry and at a certain point into the walk they would all settle down on the checked rug to drink tea, hot from flasks, sandwiches unfolded from greaseproof paper and little cupcakes that she always made on a Saturday afternoon. The boys moaned if they walked too far, the way children do, pulling at her arm, asking to rest, then hiding from her behind trees before leaping out in surprise.

She misses her boys. It has been ten years.

She stands up again and does her small walk. She does not know how many times a day she performs this ritual, but she does know that it never gets any easier.

She finds that it helps to daydream whilst she walks. Her home. Her lovely home. Her home that she spent forty years creating. The teak sideboard, its scent of oil, polish, warm wood at the back of her throat. Photos in silver frames that she arranged on its surface. Family. Her mother and father on their wedding day. Her mother's dark eyes and high forehead that she would inherit, her father's long straight nose; strong on his face, perhaps a little dominant on her own. Their expressions formal as they stood outside the church doors, her mother cradling the tiny beginnings of unknown half-lives inside her that were to become Rachael then Lillian. Rachael now lying in peace, as the expression goes, although her last few months were anything but peaceful. Lillian did her best to comfort her and even moved in for the last three weeks, but human will is nothing against God's greater wish.

She hasn't been to church for a long time now. She feels that God has turned away from her and she does not know how to ask Him to come back into her life.

She hates this part of her walk and sets her eyes straight ahead to the mountains. They look further away today, but she can make out the silver-grey rocky peaks through the haze. Tendrils of cloud drift down and filter into the ravines.

It reminds her of the dream she had last night. Michael holding her hand at the bottom of the mountain then kissing her quickly before racing up its steep incline. Not wanting to be alone, she tried to follow him and, as she struggled for footholds and scraped her palms against the rocks, she knew that she wouldn't make it without him and she called out to him, 'Michael! Wait!' But he had driven on faster and faster until he became smaller and smaller and finally disappeared over the top of the mountain. Her limbs ached, the sun burned into her scalp, but she hauled herself to the top and when she looked around she realised that she was in her own garden, the fynbos grown out of control, and as she began to wade through them to find Michael, the tangled weeds dragged her down and she felt the spiky protea leaves carve through her skin. As she stumbled, she looked up and saw Michael's face in the top window of the house and she called to him, 'Michael! Help!' but he just watched from above as she was pulled into the dense undergrowth. As she reached out an arm for him, his face began to fade into the wisps of cloud and she called his name over and over until she was hoarse and could hear nothing but the wind hitting the dense clouds which covered the mountain and now began to swirl around her and cover her as she lay in the cold damp earth, until she could see nothing but her feet then nothing but her hands, until finally she could see nothing of herself.

She sits back down and wipes her forehead. The day is hot. The black women are looking at her. She ignores them for now. She has as much right to be here as they do. The child that was sleeping on the bin bag makes its way towards her. One arm held out, palm open. Quiet, accepting eyes. She cannot tell if it is a boy or girl. Long limbs on a tiny torso, dusty green shorts and a tight grey T-shirt. She looks away from it. What is she supposed to do?

She remembers a time when there were no beggars on the street. No constant reminder that there were those less fortunate.

The sun has moved right around her from the east and she watches the yellow globe melt into the top of the mountain. She feels a shiver and pulls her anorak out from a bag under her chair. The anorak she bought twenty years ago when she and Michael decided to take a trip to the Karoo. They booked a small cottage not long after their youngest boy left for university. Lillian had heard the term Empty Nester but felt that as long as she had Michael there was nothing empty about her nest. There was just a little more room for them and, anyway, the boys would be back when they had finished their studies. She would still be required to shop and cook and tidy and organise. She had sometimes allowed herself brief thoughts of what it would be like when she was a grandmother and how she would be able to use all her skills on the next generation. But she knew it would be a while before the boys settled down.

In one hour it will be dark. She has mixed feelings about

leaving her spot, but she cannot risk being here alone in the dark. She puts the lid on the ice-cream container and packs it into her bag. She folds her deck chair and, feeling the weight in her hands, thinks about leaving it where it is, but she knows it will not be here in the morning if she does. There are always people worse off.

In one hand her deck chair, in the other her bag, around her shoulders the green anorak. The only person left on the island is the woman with her small child. They both stare at her as she walks past. Lillian holds her head high.

She steps off the island and crosses the road. She will follow it all the way to the bus stop. It is a long road.

She waits for the bus, deckchair leaning on her leg, her hand in her pocket holding the five rand it will cost her to get home.

Home. She wonders why she still uses the word. Is a home simply somewhere one sleeps? Can you call a room at the back of a liquor store home? A room with cement floors and a small barred window that looks out onto a yard of crates and boxes and a neglected Rottweiler penned in by razor wire. Where drunks collect every night, swigging from cans and bottles and swearing at each other until fights break out.

She grips her bag tighter. They will not steal it from her tonight. She will hide it under her anorak. When she gets to her room she will close her door and pull her mattress against it. She will count the coins silently, feeling each one. She will eat what is left over from last night until it is time for her to lie down and pull her blanket over her. Then, in the long hours that it takes for sleep to come to her, she will silently curse her husband for taking their boys on a hunting trip to the Karoo without her. She will silently curse the drunk driver who swerved into them on Sir Lowry's Pass, pushing their car off the road and down the mountainside.

And she will lie silently on her bed, as the noise pursues her from outside, and think of her home, her photos and her memories that were sold off to pay the debts, the hospital fees and the funeral costs.

Michael always said that life insurance was a waste of money and, in any case, he would always be there to look after her.

If she is lucky, the ice-cream box will contain enough for her to take the day off on Sunday. She is so tired these days. She just needs to sleep.

ACKNOWLEDGEMENTS

Writing these acknowledgements feels like I'm throwing a party but don't have enough time to chat to all my guests. There have been so many supportive people along the way, but I'd like to mention a few who have joined me on this specific journey.

My first thanks go to Dr Maggie Butt, my supervisor at Middlesex University, for her encouragement and belief in the early days of 'Trade', and to my MA supervisor at UCT, the late poet and professor, Stephen Watson, who taught me that one word can change the emotion of a whole page.

Thank you to my mum, Elizabeth, for being my honest reader and cheerleader. I thank my beautiful and creative daughters, Simone and Lauren (in order of appearance) for their continuous encouragement and enthusiasm. Mason, thank you for your energy and positivity and thank you, Shirley, for making sure my pencils were sharp. Kate, thank you for reading everything and for believing it was just a matter of time. Mariza, thank you for many years of mountain therapy and to Taryn and Charlotte, thank you for all your support and encouragement. To Aoife, Hazel and Sue – thank you for inspirational writing weekends and afternoons and for your friendship, guidance and support.

Thank you to Colleen Higgs for the email every writer dreams of: *We would like to publish…* Colleen gives undiscovered women writers in South Africa a platform to publish precious literary forms such as poetry, short stories and novellas, and I'm extremely proud to be part of the Modjaji Family. Thank you to Karen Jennings, who not only takes great pride in her work but edited this book with understanding, warmth and empathy. A huge thanks to Jesse Breytenbach for creating this beautiful cover.

Finally, to someone I don't even know, Elizabeth Gilbert. Her book, *Big Magic*, gave me courage; thank you, Elizabeth, for the no-nonsense talk.

★★★

'Horse' was longlisted for the Paris Literary Prize in 2011 and was published by the Novella Project in 2012.

'Bread' was published in POWA's 2012 anthology, *Breaking the Silence: Sisterhood*.

'The Story of Harap Alb' is a Romanian fairy tale, written by Ion Creanga and published in 1877.

ABOUT THE AUTHOR

Women out of Water is Sally Cranswick's debut collection of short stories. She lives in Cape Town and is a writer and workshop facilitator with a special interest in life-writing and memoir. She has an MA in Creative Writing from UCT. Before coming to South Africa, Sally lived in many countries around the world and worked as a singer in the UK and Southeast Asia.

Printed in the United States
by Baker & Taylor Publisher Services